Storm

Also by Brennig Jones

Tempest

Storm

Brennig Jones

Storm
by Brennig Jones
First published in 2024

ISBN: 978-1-7384409-0-0

Cover art © 2023 Clarabelle Clements
instagram.com/clarab3lle.artwork

Edited by @megangeorgiaediting
uk.linkedin.com/in/megan-georgia-hirst-ba29181b0

Typeset by Bittersweet
bittersweetcreations.co.uk

For Sam, Briony, Clarabelle, Louella, and all the four-legged members of my long-suffering family. Here's to many more years of suffering.

With grateful thanks to Megan Georgia, my editor of choice.

And for librarians everywhere, because they know.

Introduction

On 2nd June 1994, a British Royal Air Force Chinook HC2 helicopter, registration ZD576, flown by two RAF Special Forces pilots, took off from Aldergrove, Northern Ireland, heading for Inverness, Scotland.

It didn't arrive. Instead, it crashed on a Scottish island, resulting in the loss of all lives onboard.

There were a number of conspiracy theories about what had happened, though the official investigation stated the cause of the crash was impossible to determine. Weeks later, that ruling was overturned by two high-ranking RAF officers, who deemed the pilots responsible and decided both were guilty of gross negligence.

This is not the story of ZD576.

Margaret: Breaking up and beginning

It doesn't matter how it happens; a breakup needs to be dealt with. *You* need to deal with *it*, not the other way around. Move past the reasons it happened because, if you don't, you'll become fixated on the other person. You'll wonder what they're doing, who they're with, how they're living and that's not a good place to be. Leave all thoughts of them behind and deal with the breakup because a breakup is mostly just an ending.

You're done with it, done with them. They're done with you.

End of a chapter.

There might be some surprise at how it happened so quickly but, if you're the one who pulled the plug (and no-one has been screwing around), the breakup probably happened because you needed to go back to being the person you used to be; the person you were before you slipped beneath the relationship and into that emotional pond.

You'd slipped in willingly because you thought you were happy, right? Now, you aren't happy and that's because you've become disconnected from you. The distance between who you should be and who you've been pretending to be has been slowly growing.

Sometimes, you might catch a glimpse of the person you could be. It's like you're on a train going through a tunnel and, suddenly, there you are in the dark reflection, a different version of yourself. You look around but that other you has gone, vanished as rapidly as it had appeared, but leaving behind the half-memory of who you could be, happy and balanced.

This submerging of self started gradually in the relationship's early days when you were ridiculously happy and infatuated, so much in love that the tiniest degrees of change were hardly worth thinking about. Those changes, they didn't really matter because everything was bright and shiny and new and you only cared about them.

But lately, the almost silent voice deep inside you - the tiniest whisper in your heart - has called out to you.

You look around at your life, the soft comforts you have built, and it dawns on you those comforts have become a web of the finest emotional threads. You hadn't felt the chafing or the restriction or the misdirection. Trapped by compromise, by compassion, trapped by what you weren't... You have gradually become drawn to the direction you need to take to get back because the voice called and, with this new resolve to revert to yourself, the web fell away and the path ahead cleared.

That's how I came to live what some people call an eccentric life, because of a breakup and because I didn't want to be the person I was on the road to becoming.

But, in all this emotional turmoil, there's one thing that's true: Even an ending is a new beginning.

Chapter 1. Margaret

From my chair, I watched someone begin the long walk up the steep, grassy track. They'd come from the blue caravan down on the bend, but whoever it was, it wasn't Lisa. The unseasonably warm, late morning sun cast short shadows as it beat down. Whoever it was would be thirsty when they got to me.

I continued my crocheting while I watched them take form. She was Asian. Slight, short and, despite her clothing, she was very thin.

As she drew nearer, I noticed her head was topped by long, dark hair, worn up in a way I would never have been able to replicate. She was pretty; her face had probably broken hearts but her deep, dark eyes, much older than her late twenties, told tales of grief, suffering and pain. She looked bushed, not just tired; she looked pale, unwell and exhausted.

'Hello,' she said as she stood in front of me.

She slid out from beneath her rucksack and eased it to the ground. It was a lightly packed, aged US Army expedition pack. Fully laden, it would have been heavier than her. She wore a lightweight, desert pattern jacket that had seen serious miles. The long skirt and brightly patterned blouse underneath the jacket, were both newer than her other clothes. On her feet were a pair of well-used, military-looking boots.

She looked down at me, one knee bent as she rested after hiking up the hill. I said nothing and the silence seemed to unnerve her; the only sounds were the seagulls in the field behind, as they chased each other away from the freshly harrowed soil.

'Are you Maggie? Margaret?' She had a pleasant, quiet voice - not deep, not high-pitched - and a soft accent that could have been Canadian or American. She waited into my silence.

Without looking up, I decided to put her out of her misery.

'Forty-eight, forty-nine, fifty,' I counted aloud. I then stopped crocheting, held the work-in- progress still and looked up into her ancient eyes. 'Yes, I'm Margaret.'

'Lisa,' she said as she nodded toward the blue caravan at the foot of the ancient, grassed lane. 'She said you might advise me on the best place to pitch my tent?'

If Lisa had said that, she must have liked this girl. It was a tacit invitation to join us.

I switched my crochet to my other hand before I responded with, 'How long do you need a place for?'

'A few weeks, minimum. Maximum, three months. Maybe four.'

I looked at her while I thought about it. I wondered, because of her thinness, if she was bulimic or perhaps her illness was more aggressive? If it was, why was she looking to pitch up here?

'Well, if you're planning on staying a few weeks, there's a small copse half a mile south. It's bordered by two fields and has a stream through it so you would have fresh water. It's sheltered and you'd not be disturbed, but the farmer clears it all now and then so it's not a long-term prospect. If you want longer, you would probably be better over in Minefields.'

'Uh, Minefields?'

'Two miles away. It's a big piece of land. A couple of hundred years ago, they used to dig for minerals there, then the army used it for training until the nineteen-sixties when some ancient artifacts were dug up. It's no good for agriculture so it's turning back to a wild meadow.'

Her dark eyes seemed to churn as she thought it over.

Eventually, she asked, 'And what would you do? If you were looking to stay around here?'

'For a few weeks?' I asked, then answered. 'I'd pitch up on this lane.'

'Why?'

'We keep to ourselves but we keep an eye on each other; there's safety in numbers.'

'Safety? From who?'

'From the almost locals. The cider-heads. The angry people who feel we shouldn't be here even though *here* is not where *they* live.'

She looked puzzled and I didn't say anything more, I picked up my crochet but she interrupted me from continuing by asking the question she'd really wanted to ask.

'And where would you go if you wanted a quiet life for, say, four months?'

A quiet life for four months? I took a second to consider my response. She had a terminal illness and only a short time to live. My heart opened to her.

'Have I got any money?' I asked.

'A little.'

I thought about it for a couple of moments.

'In that case, I'd probably head to the Kennet and Avon canal. With a little money, I could pick up a narrowboat and live quietly on the water. If I didn't like it there, I'd navigate to another canal until I found the right place for me.'

I studied her eyes as she digested this unexpected advice. She didn't look like she'd finished asking questions but couldn't quite reach the next one, so I put my crochet down, sat up straight and asked if she'd like a drink. She thought about it for a moment, then politely declined. I offered her a small bottle of water for her journey which she accepted.

She loaded up her rucksack and I watched her walk further up the path. She obviously needed to go *somewhere*, even if she didn't know where that was. I watched her walk away from me.

Chapter 2. Margaret

The birds wake me before dawn. They start with one or two calling but, within a couple of minutes, they're all chirping and chirruping; the hedges and trees erupt with the racket. The Dawn Chorus is an inaccurate phrase. The birds start before the early light creeps into the sky.

I lie in bed, listening to the beautiful noise. It's a clamour I cherish, and a part of the day I feel I own.

After a while, the daylight peeps around the curtains so I slide out of bed, get dressed, pick up a blanket and an empty 5-litre water container before stepping out into the almost light. I walk up the grassy path. After 1.5 kilometres, the path widens and becomes a chalk track. I walk past the abandoned cow byres and the old, empty ruin of a farmhouse until I get to Little Willy. There, I spread my blanket and sit, leaning back against the rock. I close my eyes, empty my head and drift, despite feeling anchored to the large, neolithic stone behind my back.

These days, emptying my head is easy but it wasn't always. In the old days, I was just another cog in the wheel of modern life and, as a consequence, I'd become used to the internal clamour we all carry around inside. I had lived with it every moment of every day so how couldn't I get used to it? It was only later, after I'd changed my life, I realised the noise in my head was gradually receding and I was a becoming a better person.

After two hours of meditation, I stretch my legs, arms, and back and do some deep breathing to charge myself for the return journey. I stop at the old cow byre, refill my water container from the tap and walk home. Except, that morning, I didn't. Something wasn't right. Something felt out of alignment, and there had been just one change in the last 24 hours.

I took the footpath across the fields and headed for the copse. There was no sign of a tent this side of it. She could have built a bivouac in the woods but I doubted she had the strength for that. I turned left to walk around the wooded edge and caught a glimpse of something in the long grass ahead. I walked up to the rucksack, the one she had worn yesterday. I turned towards the woods and found her on the edge of the copse beneath a pile of bracken she'd broken off to form a shelter; unconscious, ghostly white and hardly breathing but still alive. Her hair and clothes were wet with the morning dew, her skin was icy but the pulse in her wrist beat with a slow, regular rhythm.

I rolled her over into the recovery position then jogged as well as I could across the field, back to the old cow byre. I pulled the rusty wheelbarrow out from one of the cattle pens and pushed it back to the girl. I put her rucksack in, then rolled her onto her back. I pulled her up into a sitting position, knelt down, scrambled her dead weight onto my shoulder and lifted her into the wheelbarrow. Considering there was nothing to her, she seemed heavy.

I wheeled the barrow across the field, straight to my horse-box. She didn't stir.

I left the wheelbarrow outside and jogged down the hill to Lisa's caravan. She came out, walking towards me.

'What's wrong?' she called.

'The girl,' I gasped. 'Yesterday. She's collapsed. Need you to help lift her.'

Lisa turned, told her two kids to stay in the caravan then

ran toward me. I turned and jogged back but Lisa effortlessly cruised past me.

Back at the horsebox, we lifted the girl out of the wheelbarrow and into my living room where we sat her in a chair. I put the kettle on then checked her over. Her blouse and skirt were wet through so we undressed her but left her underwear on. I rubbed her down with a towel. With Lisa's help, we lifted her onto the sofa and lay her down. I got a couple of sleeping bags out, opened them up and pulled them around her. As the kettle boiled, I gave Lisa two hot water bottles which she filled. I tucked them between the layers of sleeping bags.

'What happened?' Asked Lisa.

'She's been out in the field all night, maybe unconscious the whole time. Didn't even set up her tent. As well as everything else, she's got a touch of hypothermia.'

'Everything else?'

'I'm guessing she's ill. Did you see how thin she is? I'll check on her every twenty minutes for the next three hours. If things don't improve, I'll call for an ambulance.'

'Do you need any help?'

'I don't think so. I'll keep her warm with hot water bottles and see how she is when she wakes. If she's not too bad, she can have a shower while I make some food. She can sleep there tonight; I'll sleep in the chair.'

'*If* she stays here,' said Lisa.

'Yes, *if* she stays here but I think she will. Her pulse was strong and regular, just slower than normal. I think our girl is a fighter.'

'If you need help, come and get me.'

'I will. Thanks for your help.'

'It's what we do, right?'

'Yes,' I agreed. 'It's what we do.'

I said goodbye to Lisa then turned to watch this thin, sleeping girl, this person whose name I didn't even know.

Chapter 3: Margaret

'Hello.'

I'd dozed off. I opened my eyes and looked over at the sofa.

'Hi. How are you feeling?'

'Sleepy. Where am I?'

'In my home, where you came to talk to me yesterday. Do you remember that?'

She paused, nodded slowly then asked, 'Why?'

'Why what?'

'Why am I here?'

'I found you in the field this morning. You were unconscious. You had been out there all night. I brought you here to recover.'

'Oh.' She paused, a long and thoughtful pause. 'I'm sorry.'

'Why?'

'For causing you trouble. Sorry for… being here.'

'Oh, shush. You'll be my guest until you're strong enough to be on your way but I don't think you'll be here long.'

'No,' she said, sleepily. 'Not long.'

'Do you feel well enough to eat or drink?'

'Just some water, please?'

I filled a glass and picked up the thermometer. I don't like asking questions but I needed to know.

I stood in front of her and asked, 'How long has it been since your last fix? I saw your arms.'

She closed her eyes and looked pained.

'Months. Maybe nine or ten weeks.'

'I'm sorry but I need to know what you will be going through while you're here. You're over the worst?'

She opened her eyes and I almost shivered as her darkness seemed to touch my soul.

'Yes, I am. Thank you. I appreciate you asking. I know what I'm in for, I've been through this before.'

She put the thermometer in her mouth and I put the glass next to her before walking into the kitchen to warm some soup. I looked at her over my shoulder. She had a little more colour than when she'd walked up the hill yesterday.

'I don't know your name,' I called out.

'Shlorra,' she said around the thermometer.

'Laura?'

'Yesh.'

'I'm happy to meet you, Laura. I think you should rest today. Sleep in the big bed tonight,' I nodded to the steps behind her. 'When you need it, there's a bathroom in here,' I gestured to the doorway at the rear of the room. 'There's plenty of hot water and I think you'll feel better for a shower.'

She nodded.

'I've put a pair of pyjamas out for you. I don't have anything in your size for underwear but there's a t-shirt and a pair of shorts you can have.'

I walked back and put a mug of soup on the table next to the glass of water. She closed her eyes again and I thought I saw a tear glisten on her cheek. She handed me the thermometer and I wrote the reading on the sheet of paper with the others. Definitely over the worst of exposure but I didn't know about her opiate withdrawal. She looked so fragile and her mental state was probably in the same condition.

She opened her eyes. Yes, there had been a tear.

'Thank you.'

'You're welcome, Laura.'

She closed her eyes again so I picked up my crochet and sat silently while I added more rows. That's how most of that first afternoon went. She dozed or pretended to doze, cried to herself - sometimes in her sleep, sometimes awake - and she used the bathroom. I watched over her, carried on with my crochet and prepared small meals which she mostly left untouched.

Lisa called round. She'd brought us a loaf of bread, warm from her oven; a lovely thing to do. The day was still nice so I set up a table outside and Laura sat out with us, still wrapped in a sleeping bag. We had a simple meal - Lisa's homemade bread and my vegetable soup - but it was filling and we ate in the finest surroundings the English countryside could offer us.

Lisa and I mostly talked about her kids. Laura joined in by asking questions about them but Lisa's reticence showed; she gave Laura what information she felt comfortable with. We avoided asking Laura about her life, both of us prodding at her past might not be good for her.

When the sun began setting, Lisa said she had to check that David and the kids hadn't set fire to the caravan, and went home. Laura and I said goodnight and continued to sit outside, enjoying the last rays of the day.

After a long ten minutes of silence, she asked, 'What are you making?'

'A big, chunky cardigan for winter.'

'I like the colours, very autumnal.'

I smiled. 'These were the only colours the wool shop had in their sale.'

'And that's why you're making a winter cardigan? Because of the colours?'

'Sort of. I need a chunky winter cardigan. I damaged the last one gathering firewood a while ago.'

'In a day or two, when I'm stronger, I'll help with things like that.'

I was at the end of a row so I paused.

'I think, in a day or two, when you're stronger, you'll be getting ready to leave.' I started the next row.

Her expression told me I was right but she protested.

'Maybe I won't. Maybe I will stay nearby to repay you for your help.'

Counting quietly to myself, I smiled and nodded, though I knew she wouldn't.

After a long, reflective pause she said, 'It's so quiet here.' She made a point of looking around the countryside. 'I like that there's nothing modern here, no construction, no development.'

I finished another row. 'Two thousand years ago, the Romans came here but…' I pointed down the track. 'This road was thousands of years old even before their first ships arrived. When the summer has dried the ground out, you can see cart tracks on this ancient road. You're sitting on what is a four-thousand-year-old motorway. It stretched across all of Wessex and now? Yes, now it's quiet here but this was a big construction for the time.'

She said nothing. Maybe she was trying to imagine the

traffic that would have passed along this road four thousand years ago.

Eventually, she said, 'I love how still and quiet it is.'

I watched her as I started another row.

After a while, her head nodded forward as she drifted into sleep. I wondered who or what she was running away from.

Chapter 4: Margaret

The sun dipped below the horizon. She woke with the sudden chill so we moved inside. Laura used the bathroom and eventually emerged, freshly showered and wearing my too-large pyjamas. I apologised for not having a hairdryer. I offered her a drink and some more food. She said she couldn't eat anything else but accepted another glass of water. I showed her the double bed above the driver's cab.

'Are you sure?' she asked

'You need it more than me. I'll sleep down here.'

She looked uncertain but, when I came out of the bathroom, she was tucked in bed and either fast asleep or feigning it. I kept a light on and settled down for the night.

In the early hours, I was jerked awake when she cried out then lapsed into crying big sobs of grief and loss and longing.

I climbed the steps. She looked childlike and fragile. I checked her forehead for fever and she grasped my wrist and held it to her chest. I took the hint and climbed up onto the bed. She rolled away from me, keeping hold of my arm. I cuddled in behind her and spent an uncomfortable night while she slept fitfully.

When the early birds began their song the next morning, we were still in the same position. She felt me fidget.

'Do we get up now?'

'Soon, but not right now.'

There was a long pause before she spoke again.

'I'm sorry.'

I understood her apology.

'It's OK.'

'I've imposed on you and disrupted your life. I'm sorry for that.'

'Really, it's fine.'

'I'll go looking for a pitch today.'

'I don't think you're ready for that.'

'I feel bad and I want to get out of your hair.'

'We can talk later. Don't make a decision yet. Wait until you're up and moving about, see how you feel. We'll talk when I get back.'

'Oh? Back from where?'

'I go up the lane and meditate for a couple of hours every morning.'

'OK. Is there anything you want me to do while you're gone?'

'Yes. I want you to rest.'

The day started overcast, the heavy morning dew soaking my feet as I walked up the track. The morning sun didn't bring warmth and, by the time I got back from Little Willy, I was chilled to the bone. When you're my age, sitting with your back against an ancient stone for two hours takes its toll.

I was pleasantly surprised to see a fire burning in the

stone circle and the kettle warming. Laura was wrapped up against the cold morning air, sitting beside the fire, wrapped in a sleeping bag.

'I didn't know what you wanted for breakfast, but there's some of Lisa's bread left.'

'I think a cup of tea and some toast might be just about perfect. What would you like?'

'I'll have the same.'

Despite this agreement for action, I sat with her and, for five minutes, we watched the flames in the fire as they danced for our entertainment. When she got up from the chair, I didn't quite growl but I told her to sit and rest.

'It's lovely that you've lit the fire, but you are supposed to be taking it easy. Please, don't do chores.'

'I feel well enough.'

'Maybe you do and that's great, but you're my guest and my guests don't do chores in my home.'

I stepped inside. Laura followed me and leaned against the counter while I got breakfast ready.

'I looked at the photographs on your shelves,' she said. 'You were a handsome couple.'

'Thank you. He was handsome. I was just adequately pretty.'

'Well, that's not true. You were stunning.'

I turned to look at the pictures, even though I knew them so well.

'It was a military wedding?' she asked.

'Yes, it was a formal affair.'

'There must have been hundreds of people there.'

'A hundred and fifty but the regiment, squadron and their wives and partners made the numbers up.'

'And this photograph next to it?' She picked it up. 'Your husband in a flight suit, wearing a sidearm, leaning against a helicopter?'

'Harry was an air force pilot attached to a special army regiment. He had a lot of friends and colleagues in both services who loved him almost as much as I did.'

She put the photograph down carefully. 'Can I ask what happened?'

'He died on a flight to Scotland. Nobody has explained how it happened but he crashed.'

'I'm so sorry.'

'It was a long time ago. Nineteen-ninety-four gets further away every year.'

'I don't want to pry but how did the wife of an air force officer end up living in a wagon in the middle of nowhere?'

'When you're the wife of a military man and he dies, you lose your house. Family accommodation is there for the families of serving men and women. When Harry died, the regiment tried to keep me housed as long as they could but it was a battle even they couldn't win.'

'I'm horrified! You lost your husband and got thrown out of your home?'

'It's how it goes. I was lucky. I had this horsebox from when I used to show horses. When Harry died, I let the horses go, stripped out the horsebox and converted it.'

'And moved to the middle of nowhere.'

I smiled at her accurate description; modern civilisation is scant in these parts.

'I have an affinity with the area. Harry and I used to go down to Avebury a few times a year. I love the stones there. You can walk right up to them. I feel connected when I'm near them. There are many Neolithic and Megalithic standing stones around here, not just the well-known ones up the track,' I said, nodding in the direction of Stonehenge. 'There are stones all over the place. They mean something to me. I can't afford a house anywhere now but I can live here in the horsebox and, in some ways, I'm closer to a proper lifestyle than a lot of other people.'

I stared out of the window at the rolling countryside that I call home.

Chapter 5: Margaret

She spent one more night with me. The following day, against my advice, she left after lunch to set up her tent in the copse.

The day after she left, I called round just before 9:30, as we'd arranged. I noticed she was no stranger to camping; her tent was expertly set and well placed. There were signs of a well-tended fire from the previous night.

With little more than a casual greeting, we walked south. The footpath ran across a handful of fields and took us down to the main road where we waited for a bus.

'And you do this every week? Take a bus to Salisbury?'

'Only if I need a big shop,' I answered. 'If I need a few things, I'll walk up the footpath to Larkhill.'

'What's Larkhill like?'

'A garrison town. Dull.'

'And Salisbury?'

'A nice place slowly being destroyed by twenty-first

century life.'

'Oh.'

When the bus arrived, we climbed aboard and took our seats. We watched the countryside gradually become the outskirts of Salisbury and then get even more built-up. At the city centre bus station, we got off and walked through the old town into the main shopping areas.

I showed her the cheapest shops and the best supermarkets, the shops to avoid and the stalls to get fresh fruit and veg from. We bought enough supplies for a fortnight and walked back towards the bus station.

We were about to cross one of the many footbridges that span the streams and rivers that lace through the city when a group of five lads leaning on the railing whistled, jeered and shouted abuse at us. I'm used to it. People like me don't fit their norm and they can tell. We're targets for their outrage.

One of the lads - early 20s, large, well-built, and filled with anger and bad decisions - shouted at Laura for a blowjob. She paused then, in a single movement, slipped off her rucksack, walked up to him and quietly asked him to behave himself because there were young children around. The lad leaned over her to emphasize his height and said he'd give her a young child and the old hag could watch.

Then the strangest thing I've ever seen happened.

At almost the same moment he'd uttered his last word, this wisp of a girl had put a hand on his arm and suddenly he was on his back in the stream behind her. It was as if he'd jumped over her head. Laura hadn't even seemed to exert herself.

The rest of the group stood, slack-jawed, while she quietly told them all to behave themselves in public. Behind her, the lad in the water scrambled about madly and ran straight at her back. He was less than a metre away when, without even looking, she took a graceful pace to the side and tripped him as he ran through where she'd been. He hit the ground, face first, and stayed down. His friends crowded round and lifted him up, showing that his face was badly scratched and bleeding. Laura just turned, slipped into her rucksack and walked back to me.

'Is it this way?' she asked.

I nodded, looked over my shoulder to check nobody was coming after us and then continued to the bus station. It was a little while before I could speak.

'What on earth was that?'

'It was almost a *Morote Seoi Nage*, my favourite variation on one.'

'What is a *Morote Seoi Nage*?'

'It's a Judo throw. Nothing special.'

'I'd hate to see you do something special. He was twice your weight and a foot taller.'

'He was stupid and he was rude to you. I won't have that. You helped me without consideration when I needed help. I owe you. The least I can do today is stop someone from being rude to you and teach them never to do it again.'

'You owe me nothing.'

'You came to find me, you carried me back to your home, gave me your bed and your food and kept a watch over me all night. I owe you big time.'

'I didn't carry you; I used a wheelbarrow.'

'Whatever.' She smiled but it was clear she'd drawn a line under the conversation. We kept silent for almost the whole journey home.

We had walked up the footpath and arrived at her pitch. I was preparing to say goodbye when she put her shopping down, turned to me and said the most unexpected thing.

'I don't believe that nobody knows what happened. To your husband, I mean. I know someone who could make enquiries, if you really wanted to know?'

It was as if I felt the earth shift beneath my feet.

'I… I don't know. It was so long ago.' I was almost speechless. She'd thrown open a door that I didn't know existed. 'He was my husband. I loved him so much and, in a way, I still miss him but what good would it do to go through dusty, old files now?'

'It could give you an answer to what happened. It could give you the kind of closure that you haven't had. It might give you an understanding, if you wanted that?'

My head was a whirlpool; my heart, a tumult of emotion. I needed to think. It had taken me years but I'd come to a kind of peace over Harry's death. I'd changed my life and I wasn't the same person anymore. Did I want to reopen those old wounds?

She reached out and gently touched my arm in a way that reminded me of the Judo throw, though I didn't go spinning over her head.

'I can see you need to think about this. Take your time. Mull it over.'

'It's just so… unexpected. After all this time.'

'I hope I haven't upset you,' she said as she released my arm.

'No, not upset, just… I feel like I've had the breath knocked out of me.'

'I'm sorry, that wasn't my intention. I wanted to do something for you after everything you've done for me.'

'You've already done something for me. Today.'

'That was nothing. I wanted to do something real, something tangible, something that you can carry with you for a long time.'

I felt dazed. 'I need to think. There's so much to consider.'

'Take your time. I'll be here when you've decided.'

I turned and walked up the footpath. Once back home, I put the kettle on, sat in my favourite chair and picked up my crochet but the hook stayed still.

Chapter 6: Margaret

I slept badly that night. My brain hopped around and gave me no peace. The violence that Laura meted out troubled me and the scene kept playing in my head.

Then there was her offer to find out more about Harry's death. Two big things to occupy my head and keep me awake. And they did.

Some might say the lad deserved some kind of telling off but what happened was shocking. I'm not accustomed to violence.

I couldn't get my head around the way she just dealt with him, as casually as I would peel an orange. There was no pause, no discussion, not even a threat. It was instant, so quick that, even as I replayed it, I couldn't believe the speed of it all. She'd dealt with him as if he was inconsequential, as if she could barely be bothered to consider him a threat.

That all this happened in the middle of Salisbury made it more unreal and Laura had behaved as if nothing much had transpired.

What would Harry have made of it? He worked with people who were used to physical violence. Would he have approved of what Laura did? Harry was a gentle man but he had been trained to fight. That thought made me slightly comfortable but, at the same time, it troubled me because it was a sign of how different my life had become.

Was I so changed that I didn't want to delve into Harry's accident? Did I want to open a new window into the place I'd left far behind? Time hadn't dimmed my memories but, since he'd been gone, I had changed and shifted my entire lifestyle. I'd left the cosy world of 'normal' behind, just as I had left other people for this solitary, nomadic life.

In the space of a few days, Laura had made ripples in my life. Little ripples in the grand scheme of things, maybe, but I now felt as if I was being swamped.

I still thought about Harry. I thought about him every day. I don't know if that was part of grieving or if I had moved beyond that. Was I keeping the memories going as a way of keeping Harry alive or was it just habit?

Only a few days ago, my memories had drifted through the crazy weekend we'd spent in the Malvern Hills. We had driven all over the countryside in Harry's little sports car and stopped at a pub on the Welsh border for dinner. We'd stayed in a B&B with a squeaky bed; springs so noisy we lay on towels in the bathroom to make love. I loved my memories but they were just that: Memories. Did I want to taint them by being told how or why he died?

Meeting and then marrying Harry were things I was prepared for, life events I had been sort of programmed for from an early age. They were changes I accepted with all the willing eagerness and unconditional love of a young bride. I had little experience of life outside of school and university, where we'd met.

Being a military wife also brought changes I accepted, changes which Harry eased. I knew he was going to be a military pilot when he'd completed his degree; that was a change Harry made easy for me. When he'd completed his training and was posted to the army base in Hereford, Harry and I settled into an easy sort of married military life. The training exercises he had to go away for came frequently but were always brief. He never saw action but he and his colleagues trained all the time.

When he died, I was devastated.

Well, no. At first, I was numb. The drugs the doctor gave me softened everything. There were no physical, mental or emotional sharp edges for me to bump into. I was cocooned. His colleagues came and helped me when they could, helped me through the coroner's hearing and, later, they helped me through the military hearing. I was numb to it all. They helped me when I had to move out of family accommodation.

When I came off the prescription drugs, I bumped into all the sharp edges. Everything hurt and it got worse every day for a long time. The man I truly loved, the one human being I was devoted to… was no longer in my life.

Now, Laura was asking if I wanted to open up old wounds, old memories. Did I want to spend more time in the past than I already had? I thought those old wounds had healed but there I was, wide awake at God knows what time it was. I was confused and hurting all over again. The longer I thought about it, the more I wondered if I had actually gotten over Harry's death at all. Decades had passed and, yet, I was still hurting.

I lay awake and all I achieved was frustration and a lack of sleep.

Early the next morning, I walked up the track and leaned back onto Little Willy. I felt the warmth of the sunrise on my face and tried to clear my head but, no matter how hard I tried to empty my thoughts, I couldn't stop the mental traffic. Unable to relax, I got more frustrated.

After a while, I felt my frustration transform into an emotion I hadn't felt for a long time.

I got angry.

I detoured on the way home. My sandaled feet seemed to soak up the morning dew from the entire field as I walked down the footpath and, irrationally, that made me angrier.

She was sitting on her rucksack beside the fire, a pan of water just starting to boil.

'I thought you might like a cup of tea?'

'No, thank you,' I said.

'I'd offer you a seat but I don't have a seat to offer you.'

'I'll stand anyway. This won't take long.'

'Maybe long enough for you to have some tea?' I watched her pour the hot water into two metal mugs and add teabags. 'You're angry,' she said.

'I… I… I… It's just…' I couldn't get the words out. I tried not to look like a fish out of water, gasping for breath while I attempted to speak again. 'No, I'm not angry. I'm furious more than angry. I feel like I'm boiling over.'

'And it's because of me.'

'Yes, it's because of you.'

'Because I woke something inside you.'

I started to feel uncomfortable, like I didn't have control over this conversation. 'Yes, you messed with something inside me. How is it you know these things?'

'You don't hide your feelings.'

I looked down at her. 'The tea?'

'I heard you coming. Your footsteps sounded angry.'

'You heard me coming through the long grass and you could tell I was angry?'

'I have good hearing.'

'And you know I'm angry because you've woken something inside me?'

'Process of elimination. I didn't think it was because I threw that guy into the stream. So, it had to be what I said to you, what I said about your husband.'

'It was,' I said.

'I touched a nerve and I woke something that's been sleeping deep inside you for a long time.'

'Rage,' I said. 'You woke my rage.'

'So, I think we need to do something about that. Would you like some tea while we talk?'

'Has anyone ever said you can be infuriating?'

She smiled up at me.

Chapter 7: Margaret

The next day, we took the bus into Salisbury. A second trip so soon after the last one was an extravagance but Laura said she needed some supplies so I accompanied her.

She bought a cheap mobile phone. We sat on a bench in

the park while she set it up then she handed it to me.

'What's this for?'

'Comms so we can stay in touch. I'll use the messaging app because it's encrypted. Don't use the phone for anything else except for messaging me. I've disabled GPS. Don't switch that on.'

'Are you going somewhere?'

'Yes,' she said. 'I'm going to ask someone to get some information for you.'

'Can't you do that from here? Ask them, I mean? Email them or something?'

'This needs to be a face-to-face conversation.'

'In that case, I don't want you to do it. I don't want to be any bother.'

'We talked about this yesterday. It's something I can do for you. You have pushed your rage down inside; buried a part of you. Yesterday, it was your rage that drove you to say we should find out more information.'

'Yesterday, I let my rage out. Today, it's gone away.'

'It hasn't gone away,' she said. 'You've pushed it down inside again.'

'I think I'm happy with it being there.'

She sighed, turned to face me and held my gaze with her bottomless eyes. 'You're hiding the rage and you're hiding from it. You are masking what you really want. You were angry yesterday and you directed that anger at me but we both know I'm not the source of your rage, don't we?'

I said nothing because she was right.

'And you know that masking things is going to come back and bite you, sooner or later.'

I said nothing again.

'Look on the bright side: You've got a new phone and I won't be gone long, maybe a couple of weeks.'

I didn't know what to say so instead I kept saying nothing.

'Let's do a little shopping. Would you like one of those fruity teas we had the other day?'

'No.' I tried not to sound like a sullen teenager but it came out like that anyway.

'How about some ice-cream? Or would you like some sweets?'

'You do know that I'm old enough to be your grandmother? You're being very patronising.'

'Age is what you feel, not numbers on a calendar.'

'Only a very young person could say that.'

'I'm older than I look.'

'No,' I said. 'I'm older than *you* look.'

'Maybe you just look older than I am.'

'That's meaningless nonsense. Anyway, why are we talking about age?'

'I don't know. You started it.'

'You're supposed to be respectful of your elders,' I said.

'There you go, talking about age again.'

'You can be infuriating.'

'You said that yesterday. Anyway, it's been said before. So, fruity tea?'

'We'll pick one up on the way to the bus station.'

We did. The walk back to the bus was uneventful but, as we boarded, I noticed the young man Laura had thrown into the stream. He was staring at us from the top of a double-decker in the next bay. His face was bruised, blue and black, and the grazes down his face looked painfully swollen. He didn't look happy to see us but Laura didn't notice he was there.

After the bus dropped us at our stop, we crossed the fields, briefly stopping at Laura's tent then walking down to my lorry. As I opened the door, she rummaged in her jacket pocket and pulled out a small box of teabags.

'I have a gift,' she said.

'I don't want any gifts.'

'I thought you'd say that so I'm just going to leave this box of fruity teabags here.' She placed the small, brightly coloured box on my chair outside.

'Didn't I say you can be infuriating yesterday?'

'I can be infuriating every single day of the year. Anyway, you said it earlier too.'

I exhaled slowly.

'Stay for tea. I've got a casserole almost ready and you're welcome to share it.'

'Thank you, that would be great.'

I set the meal to finish cooking while we sat outside. I worked on my crochet and drank some tea. Laura had a glass of water and read one of my seed catalogues.

'Is there really something called Perpetual Spinach? Because that's a weird mental image.'

'It makes a very nice addition to a salad.'

'And Giant Exhibition Longpod is really a real thing you can eat?'

'Beans,' I said. 'But not of the baked kind.'

'The Sutton Dwarf? That just sounds wrong, like a very short person from Sutton.'

'Another bean. I grow those.'

'Where is your garden?'

I sighed at the interruption, set down my crochet and walked her to the gap in the hedge behind us.

'It's not much.' I gestured to my 2 by 5 metre plot. 'It's just a little bit of the verge of a fallow field. I dug it out when I moved here. It's big enough to grow some beans, potatoes, onions and lettuce. I share what I harvest with whoever is around at the right time. There's also wild garlic in the hedge and the blackberrying was good last season.'

I don't know if she was impressed. Out of everyone I'd ever met, Laura was the most difficult person to read but she looked at the garden and seemed interested.

Chapter 8: Margaret

The evening meal was pretty good. I'm not a bad cook. Harry never complained about my food except in jest. At least, I think it was in jest. I was happy to see Laura finish her bowl and eat all the bread I had put aside for her. She seemed physically stronger than when she'd walked up the hill a few days before. Mentally, something was different about her. It was as if she'd found a focus.

I'd expected her to have an appetite like a bird but she tucked into the food on her tray.

Later, after I'd cleared away the dishes, I sat beside the fire with her. Dusk had begun to gather around us.

We watched the flames while I crocheted. Eventually, she spoke. 'I'm curious, Margaret, how did you end up living in a horsebox on the hippy trail within sight of Stonehenge?'

'I told you, I had to move out of family accommodation.'

She gave me a smile. 'You did, yes, but that's not how you got *here*. Something happened between then and now.'

I didn't answer.

'Am I being too nosey?' she asked.

I didn't answer some more.

'Or are you counting?'

After a couple of beats, I said, 'If I ever finish this cardigan, it's going to be so lopsided I'll never be able to wear it. I'm going to call it Laura, in honour of the person who made me lose count so often.'

'Do you name all your clothes?'

'Yes. My favourite bra is called Peter Shilton.'

'Why?'

'He was a goalkeeper, famous for having huge hands.'

'You're joking?'

'Yes, I am.'

'You're joking with me as a way of not answering my question?'

'You have good skills, Laura. You should work with people.'

'I have done,' she said. 'I don't like some people. I do like others.'

'Have you met a lot of people?'

'More than you have,' Laura said.

'I doubt that.'

'Anyway, here you are, not answering my question again.'

I sat still, just breathing the cooling evening air.

'You don't have to answer,' she said softly.

I surprised myself. 'John the Bastard,' I said.

'I'm sorry?'

I paused before going on. I hadn't told anybody this story and yet I was about to tell this strange girl everything. It was odd that I felt so comfortable talking to her.

I closed my eyes and started talking again.

'About two years after Harry died, I was living in a small, rented flat in Hereford when I had a relationship with John the Bastard and, yes, I never should have done that and, no, I'm not proud of myself. Ordinarily, I wouldn't have. He wasn't my type in any kind of way but he had a kind of magnetism. He was attractive and confident and a charmer and I was so uncertain of myself. I was going through a very low patch; I didn't know my place in the world and I was so lonely and…' I paused for breath. 'Well, I suppose I was vulnerable.'

I had opened the floodgates; the words came out in a torrent.

'It started normally. We met through a friend of a friend of a friend. He was witty and funny and attentive. Never once did he cross any lines. He was just company. He said he understood the pain I'd gone through. He took me out and entertained me. He wined and dined me and he was so funny and, to be honest, Laura, I hadn't done any laughing for so long… After a few months - don't judge me, please - but, after a few months, we became lovers and I enjoyed the physicality because I'd missed that too. He was passionate and, God, two years is such a long time and suddenly all the physical love I wanted was right there. He was a good talker too. He spoke about his place in South Africa and how he would retire there one day and just enjoy being happy in a warm climate. It sounded idyllic.'

I hesitated before delving deeper into this walled-off memory.

'I don't know when he changed or when I changed or when *we* changed but, whatever change happened, it happened so gradually that I barely noticed. We slipped into a different kind of relationship, one where I didn't have to think or make decisions and I stopped being me. I suppose it was like boiling a frog. You know, if you put a frog in a pot of boiling water, it will jump straight out but, if you put a frog in a pot of cold water and gradually heat it up, it'll stay there and die. I think that part of my life, my time with John the Bastard, was like slowly boiling a frog.'

I paused, took a sip from my drink and gave Laura a hard look. To her credit, she seemed interested in my tale so I continued.

'Gradually, he became controlling in a subtle kind of way and I didn't see it. We were well into the relationship when I realised that I wasn't making my own decisions or living my own life. At the time, I was still adjusting to being a widow and I didn't know what *my* life was supposed to be so it was easy to drift into the wrong kind of life. I don't know what the trigger was but, one day, I realised what was going on and it was like I had woken up. I had to get out. I had to walk away and not give him any way back into my life. I blocked him from my accounts, left him a voicemail to say it was over then switched off my phone and went to stay with a former colleague of Harry's in the on-base family accommodation. A week later, I went down to Devon and spent a few nights in a grotty little B and B. Staying there made me feel sad and cold and lonely, so I drove to the livery yard where I kept my horsebox. My horses had already gone to new owners, but the living accommodation in the horsebox was a good refuge. It was my place, not someone else's. I had made some happy memories in there. The kitchen was basic but I could eat a meal, the bed was comfortable and the bathroom was adequate.

'The fortnight I lived in the horsebox was a catalyst for me. I started making plans to strip it out, insulate the lorry, fit solar panels on the roof and expand the living space to fill the length of the lorry. I wanted to make it into a proper mobile home. Finishing with John the Bastard was when I got my life back. I just wished I hadn't submerged myself in him first.'

I sat still. It was like I'd opened a box of emotions and poured it all out for us to pick over my horrible mistakes. The atmosphere felt thick.

Laura cleared her throat.

'Blocked him from your accounts?'

'He was a kind of accountant, good with numbers. I had given him access to my savings and investments and bank account.'

'Ah.'

'There's nothing like an old fool, Laura, and I'm an old, old fool.'

'Did you lose money?'

'Almost everything.'

'I'm so sorry.'

'Don't be. It got me here. I've spent decades living in this lorry. We've had a good time.' I patted the side panel and looked at my modest quarters, grateful for the safety and comfort it afforded me. 'We've lived all over southern England and I've enjoyed it all. After everything that's happened, I think I have found what - and where - my life is supposed to be. I feel comfortable in this life, Laura. This is a good life.'

I looked at her and saw a hint of something in her eyes. The flash of whatever it was quickly vanished but there had been something going on inside her head.

Dusk was turning to darkness when we said goodnight. I offered Laura my bed but she said she'd go back to her tent. I put another log on the fire and watched her walk up the track.

I slid the kettle onto the grate and leaned back in my chair to gaze at the stars. The night sky is the best show on the planet; it never fails to amaze me. There's so much beauty and wonder up there, and so much we don't know.

After a while, the kettle began to whistle. I poured hot water into a mug, wrapped my shawl around my shoulders and stargazed some more. I saw a string of satellites and what might have been the International Space Station. The lights of a high-altitude aircraft twinkled as it passed overhead and the stars shone brighter as the sky darkened.

A couple of hours later, not long after midnight, I was watching the Milky Way take shape when I heard the first cry. It was a way off, not close but not far. I held my breath.

A few moments later, I heard it again. Not a fox nor a badger and it didn't sound like deer.

I took shallow breaths.

The next cry was louder, more prolonged but not any closer.

There was a sob, a loud, crying sob followed by a heavy silence. I wondered what animal would make such sounds. The quiet seemed to close in around me and I heard nothing else. I stayed outside for another hour then buried the fire, climbed the step into the lorry and locked up.

Later, I heard the distant two-tone of emergency services. A fire somewhere, maybe, or someone going to hospital in Salisbury. I hoped whoever it was would be alright.

I searched for sleep but it wouldn't come so I got out the phone that Laura had given me, opened the messaging app and sent a brief message. Then, I rolled over and tried for sleep again.

Chapter 9: Laura

I'd seen the thug on the top deck of the bus from our coach. He looked angrier than when he'd pulled himself out of the stream. How could someone so young be so full of hatred? When our bus pulled out onto the road, I checked over my shoulder and he wasn't on the top deck anymore. A minute or so later, a taxi dropped in behind and followed us out of Salisbury.

As we got off at our stop, the taxi drove past and pulled in a little distance along the road. We crossed over, climbed the style and headed up the footpath towards my camp. I saw him clumsily following us while trying to conceal himself.

Margaret is a sensitive person, gentle, fragile and easily upset. I knew she was troubled by the way I'd dealt with things in Salisbury and I wanted to avoid upsetting her again. I'd already pushed too hard by offering to find information about Harry's death but I owed her a lot for looking after me. In my world, people who help others, unasked and with no expectation of reward… Well, those people are precious.

Much later, when I got back from Margaret's lorry after tea, I circled around the copse. He had gone but the long grass where he'd stood was still flattened. He would have guessed the small tent was mine and I was certain he would come for me. I was also certain he wouldn't come alone.

I'd already figured out how his mind worked. Attacking a defenceless, young woman from behind in broad daylight and in a public place was apparently nothing so it wasn't unreasonable to think he would come back when I was asleep. He would be brutal. He was powered by hatred, anger and the irrational envy of anything that didn't fit his norm. He wouldn't come alone because he was looking to inflict maximum damage.

I reckoned they'd come at midnight or just afterwards. That gave me four hours. I walked to my tent, packed my belongings and carried my pack down to the main road. I stowed it near the style, slid beneath the hedge and settled in for a long wait. I lay on my back and tried to watch the darkening sky but there was too much light pollution this close to the road. I dozed.

Just after midnight, I heard the sound of a small car crunching over the gravel as it pulled into the layby. Five men got out. I waited until they'd all climbed over the style. It was a dark, moonless night but I could pick out their shapes against the headlights of the occasional late-night traffic as it sped along the road.

They single-filed up the footpath, using mobile phones as torches. I waited until they'd passed me then approached from behind. I dropped the last one in the line with a kick between his legs. He didn't say much but the 'oooof' was enough to attract attention. I stepped sideways and forward and rabbit-punched the next one on the back of his neck as he half turned, then moved on a pace and crouched before he even started to drop.

The third was unable to see me but he'd worked out

something was wrong. He turned towards where he thought someone was going to be which put him parallel with me. I sprang up, roundhouse punched him in the middle of his face then side-kicked him with a *Yoko Geri*, a Karate kick that makes maximum use of your opponent's weight being in the wrong place at the wrong time. He flew away from me and landed hard against the wooden fence. I dropped into another crouch.

The two who were still upright had nothing going for them. I straight-armed the next guy in the testicles then I reached behind his head with both hands and threw him into the ground, face first. I rolled away and crouch-ran back to the style.

The last man standing was cutting out, heading back towards the main road. I could tell from his size and shape he was the man who had tried to attack me in Salisbury. He flashed his phone as he moved towards the style.

I waited until he was halfway over before I hooked his left leg from underneath him. He dropped hard, the wooden crossbar catching him between his legs. As he fell, I pulled him back into the field and kicked his already damaged face. On top of his injuries from yesterday, that was going to hurt. Then, I kicked him in the face again, just for the way he'd insulted Margaret.

I picked up my pack, stepped over his unconscious body and climbed over the style to the road. I was going to Devizes to find somewhere for breakfast and then I was going shopping for a narrowboat. I always followed good advice.

Chapter 10: Margaret

After reaching a decision in the night, I felt I needed to put distance between me and Harry, some space between the past and the present.

I had breakfast and then I cleaned. I scrubbed the windows, handwashed the curtains, cleaned the grill and the oven. After a break for tea, I did the carpets and rugs and then changed the bed linen.

By lunchtime, I had nothing else to do except crochet and watch the curtains as they dried on the washing line. I'd been putting off those jobs for a while and getting them done gave me a feeling of accomplishment as well as being therapeutic. I took tea and crackers outside and started on the cardigan's sleeves. I'd have it finished in two or three days.

I ate my lunch and looked over the countryside, thinking how lucky I was to live this lifestyle. By mid-afternoon, I had finished the left sleeve. I still didn't want to go and see Laura.

I put my crochet down and walked north-east up the footpath for an hour. I came to the 2,300-year-old site of Woodhenge. I enjoyed the peace and quiet as I sat on one of the small, concrete posts that marked where the wooden posts had originally been. I sat in silence, alone with my thoughts.

I decided that I loved the solitude so much that I was going to avoid Laura tomorrow. She hadn't been a difficult person to be around, I just enjoyed my own company more than hers.

Chapter 11: Laura

Her name was Karlee which, I was told, was a portmanteau of Karen and Lee, the names of the couple who first owned her. She was an eight-year-old, steel-built narrowboat in good condition. Outside, she was painted a tasteful shade of dark green with some bright daffodil motifs. Inside, she was mostly stripped pine. She came fully furnished and, the agent said, if I didn't want any bells or whistles added, I could motor her away as soon as my payment hit his account.

We shook hands on it and, ten minutes later, I owned a 45' narrowboat. The agent arranged for someone to spend the next day aboard, showing me everything from how to light the log burner to how to drive, moor and maintain the boat.

The day after that, stocked with fresh water and a decent supply of food, I cast off from the canal bank and pointed Karlee westwards towards the site of the ancient Roman city of Aquae Sulis.

As I stood in her stern, hand on the tiller, listening to the engine *putter-putt*, I firmed up my thinking for Margaret. I reckoned I could get this sorted in one cycle. I had other lines of enquiry running but there was no reason I couldn't handle multiple investigations at the same time.

I knew that pre-computer British military records are difficult to work through. Most of the paper files haven't been digitised, they sit in secure storage in the West of England. I didn't know the right people to unlock such things and the trick with investigations like this was to get someone else to do the legwork.

I knew a guy who used to work in British army intelligence. I was pretty sure he would be helpful. But my enquiry agent of choice was going to be the British MOD themselves.

I probably needed to get into the Whiteland Security Company Operations Centre (which doesn't exist) in Nebak, Saudi Arabia (both of which do). From Nebak, I could mount enquiries through the US Department of Defence - which Whiteland are attached to - directly to the British MOD. I would be able to route my queries through The Pentagon or the US National Security Agency. If I needed the extra clout, I could push an enquiry through the White House Military Office.

As it looked like there was a connection to South Africa, I felt I should route a few enquiries through to South Africa's National Intelligence Agency.

I decided to get things moving as soon as I was in place in the next cycle. It would take a while but that was OK. I'd still need to hold back the results until week 34 or later to fit into Margaret's timeline. She wouldn't know me in the next cycle but I'd cross that bridge when I came to it.

Meanwhile, in this one, I had 19 weeks left to run, 19 weeks in which to kick back and enjoy myself before it started all over again. I was going to get a more relaxed challenge in the next cycle.

I liked Margaret. She was a good, kind and gentle soul who had been short-changed in life. I wanted to do something she would appreciate.

I mulled everything over as I listened to the gentle soundtrack of the engine and watched the picture-perfect English countryside drift slowly past.

19 weeks of this would be relaxing.

Chapter 12: Margaret

I don't get visitors and it's not only because I like it that way. People who live in converted horseboxes on ancient rights of way far out in the countryside don't get folks dropping by for a chat or a cup of tea. Usually, passers-by ignore us or give us a very wide berth.

Yet, in the space of three weeks, I've had one visitor and, looking up the track, was about to get two more. Three visitors in three weeks is three visitors more than I've had in the last few years, not counting occasional drop-ins from Lisa or members of her brood.

First, there had been Laura. Did she count as a visitor when I brought her back in a wheelbarrow? Yes, I decided she did. She had walked up the track to me.

In a few moments time, two uniformed police officers were going to come calling or perhaps they were going to walk past me and go down the track? Either way, this old road was seeing more traffic than it had for a decade and a half.

I kept on crocheting my cardigan.

'Good morning,' said the older of the two as they approached. The younger was a woman.

I wondered if they were going to try to clear us out. It's been tried before.

The woman gave my box a good look over and I saw her write down the registration number. She was probably going to check if it was road legal. The older one did introductions while she wrote in her notebook.

'I'm Constable Stevens and this is Constable Michaelson. We're making general enquiries to see if people heard anything unusual two nights ago.' The way it was phrased wasn't a question, it was a subtle invitation into a conversation. The experience of age over youth. His use of the word 'general' was good and I wondered if he'd rehearsed his opening gambit on their way down the track.

'I don't think so. What does "unusual" mean?'

The female officer stood apart from the male but was interested in the surroundings. I guessed she was looking for signs of illegal activity.

'Well, anything really. Anything odd,' said Stevens. 'For example, did you hear or see a large group of men come through here late at night?'

'Hare coursers? They're not welcome here.'

'Would they be so unwelcome that a group of people who live on this track might have set upon them and beat them up?'

I managed to avoid rolling my eyes.

'I'm always beating people up. Ask anyone. I'm renowned for it. The battling granny, that's what they call me.' Michaelson smirked; I went on. 'Famous for beating people up, especially hare coursers. So is Lisa down the road. She's always beating up blood sports people.'

He did smile, bless him. He hadn't had his sense of humour completely extinguished by the job.

'I'm sorry, I didn't phrase that very well, Miss...'

'Todd. Margaret Todd.'

'Would there be other people on this old road who might have taken action against a bunch of men?'

'There's Lisa down the hill. She has a cutting tongue about her and her kids can be right buggers but we're all who are here right now.'

He looked thoughtful for a moment so I asked my question.

'Would you like to tell me what's happened?'

He considered what he could tell me.

'Two nights ago, just after midnight, five men were attacked and badly beaten a couple of fields away from here. Two of them are still in hospital, one is in a coma.'

I tried not to look shocked and asked the obvious question.

'What were five men doing a couple of fields away from here at midnight?'

'We've been told they were on a night march. One of them is a former soldier. He said he was training them.'

I wondered if this attack was related to the peculiar animal noises I'd heard. I felt sick that people were being beaten up and I did nothing about it.

'Wh… Where did this happen?' My voice was shaky.

'Down by the main road, near the layby.'

'Oh. We climbed over the style there on our way back from shopping the day before yesterday.'

'"We"?' He was quickly on my unguarded comment.

'A girl I went into town with. She's got a tent over that way.' I was uncomfortable bringing Laura into the conversation.

'A girl? Ah, well.' He was instantly dismissing the thought that a girl could have caused such damage to five men but, after watching Laura throw a large lad through the air with ease, I wasn't so sure.

'Perhaps she could have heard something. Can you tell me where I can find her?' he asked innocuously.

Oh God, what have I done? Regardless of whether I thought she had anything to do with it, I didn't want police officers to turn up at Laura's tent saying I'd sent them. Oh, hell! What to do?

'She's a few fields over. I'll take you but she might not like you turning up.'

He looked at me for a moment, trying to determine if there was a hidden message in what I'd said.

'That would be very kind, thank you.' At least, he had manners.

I cleared a few things away and we walked up the track, turned left through the gate before the cow byre and walked through the long grass, down to the copse where Laura's tent wasn't.

'Oh! She's not here.'

The ground where her tent had been pitched was flattened and the little stone ring where she'd built her fire held only damp-looking ash.

Michaelson bent down and touched a firestone.

'Stone cold,' she said.

'Did she mention she might be moving on?' asked Stevens.

'No.'

'No signs of a struggle,' said Michaelson.

'I agree,' he said. 'It looks like she's packed up and moved on.' He turned towards me. 'When did you get back from your shopping trip?'

I gave him the approximate time and then added, 'But she came straight back to mine. We had tea together.'

'And then she came back here, broke camp but hadn't told you she was moving on?'

'No, but some of us just move on when it's time.'

'Do you think she felt it was time?'

'No. Well, I don't know. I'm not sure. We got called names and were shouted at in town.'

He took a deep breath, slowly exhaled and sharpened his

concentration.

'Care to tell me about that?'

'A bunch of lads - cider-heads - shouted abuse and rude things at us.'

'Does that happen often?'

'Not often and not rarely. Somewhere in between.'

He pushed at a small twig with the toe of his boot and then continued.

'The thing is, Miss Todd, there are a few things that concern me. Firstly, the location where the five lads were beaten up is less than a quarter of a mile from where your friend was camped. Secondly, this place is isolated. There's nothing around here. No pubs, farms, houses; nowhere that attackers might have come *from*. Thirdly, from their injuries, I would suggest they were attacked by a superior number of people and I'd certainly say they were attacked by people who are violent and trained in administering violence. Your friend here,' he pointed at the former campsite. 'She would have heard the fight, I'm certain of that. I'm wondering if she heard the commotion, got scared and ran away?'

'Or she could have been discovered by whoever beat up the five lads and been taken away by them?' said the female officer.

I looked at her in horror. The male officer read my expression.

'I'm not sure that's likely, Michaelson. This,' he waved his hand at the flattened grass. 'This is too neat for that. The main thing I'm concerned about is she may have been frightened and run away.' He turned back to me. 'Do you have any contact details for her, Miss Todd? I'd like to make sure she's safe.'

'No. No, I don't. We don't usually socialise much. We live quiet, solitary lives.'

'I see. You wouldn't have a mobile number for her in case there was any trouble on the track?'

'No. I didn't know her that well.'

'But you went shopping with her?'

'We both needed food.'

'And she stayed most of the evening at your home and ate with you?'

A couple of simple questions and he had me. I just stood there and said nothing. He knew I was lying and I was upset she'd gone. I was angry she'd gone.

I didn't really know what to think.

Chapter 13: Laura

Travelling in a narrowboat is everything the blogs and the guidebooks tell you; it's peaceful, relaxing, picturesque. It's also very slow. It's not dull because, just like ocean sailing, you have to keep a good eye out all the time, to be aware of your surroundings and stay on top of everything. If you take your mental eye off the narrowboat ball, you'll run into that bridge or you'll take that corner at the wrong angle or you'll get too close to that half-submerged branch floating down the middle of the cut. The amount of concentration you need is bizarre given the plodding pace of travel.

So, what you do is give yourself something to look forward to while your forebrain is concentrating on all the things it needs to. You build little ripples of enthusiasm around what you're going to do when you moor for the night. You anticipate each simple activity, such as putting the kettle on and sitting down with a warm drink. You think about putting your feet up and reading another chapter in that book. The anticipation of these things feeds a gentle sense of impatience that grows inside you.

The pleasures of the positively banal activities you can't usually do when helming a narrowboat singlehandedly are somehow magnified by the slow pace of your journey. I'd been looking forward to a few things for a couple of hours when I decided to stop for the night.

I'd found a good long stretch of canal with no other boats tied up. I'd moored, more or less skilfully (it's not easy to do when you're by yourself), and double-checked the lines. Then, I did the one thing that I was looking forward to more than anything else: I switched off the engine. I was instantly enveloped in silence. My eardrums felt assaulted by the peace and quiet and I relished every second of it.

I hunkered down in the stern of the boat and watched a couple of ducks swimming about, searching for something to eat. The late afternoon sun was warm on my face. I thought that, in the morning, I might have windburn.

There was a nearby splash as a fish jumped for a fly and landed back in the water. The pastoral sounds were beautiful after hours of listening to the engine.

There was a tightness in my pocket. My phone. It reminded me of the mobile phone I'd bought with Margaret. I switched it on for the first time since I'd left the copse, half expecting it to say it couldn't find a network but being pleasantly surprised when it showed a full-strength signal. There were two messages. I read the first.

Yes, please. Find out what you can.

That was it, that was the go-ahead to look into Harry's accident. I smiled because now I had something I could do for her, something I could do to repay her kindness. I opened the second message and it took my breath away.

Laura? It's me, Margaret. I've just had two police officers visit, asking where you are and if you are OK. And if you heard any noise because five men got attacked and one of them is seriously ill in hospital and are you alright because I'm concerned for you? Please let me know you're OK and where you are. I won't tell the police, I just need to know you're alright. Why didn't you tell me you were going?

I was surprised that two police officers had been sent out to investigate the fight. I wondered if the local police were usually that diligent, or if one of the men had 'connections'.

It wouldn't matter what I told Margaret because the next time we met, she wouldn't remember this conversation, but I didn't want her to worry in the meanwhile, so I gave her the truth. Sort of.

I hit reply and composed a response.

Hi, Margaret. I meant to tell you that I needed to leave but I didn't want to upset you. This is one of those occasions when saying the right thing might come out wrong but I felt I'd wounded you when I said I might be able to get some information about your husband's crash. Perhaps I caused bad memories to surface? Good, kind, gentle people like you are treasures, gifts to the rest of us. I saw pain in your eyes and I'd put it there. I'm so sorry but I'm glad you said yes. I packed up my little camp when I got back from yours and I was gone before it got fully dark so whatever happened must have occurred after I'd left? Anyway, I'm going to follow your advice, navigate the canal.

If you need anything from me, please let me know.

Hugs & love, Laura xxx

I spent the next few months slowly cruising. The narrowboat and I eventually found the city of Bath. I picked a good mooring, a 20-minute walk down a steep hill into the centre of the city.

Bath surprised, delighted and disappointed me, all in equal measure. The architecture was pleasing and the city was neat and tidy but, in places, it felt soulless. The surrounding countryside was gorgeous to explore and I walked up and down the many hills.

Three days before I started a new cycle, I checked the phone for the last time. There were two voicemails.

Margaret sounded weak and reedy and her messages concerned me. The second voicemail made me furiously angry. I had not been so mad for years. Lisa's voice ignited in me a strong need to get back to Margaret and make things right but I only had three days left.

It was too late to do anything to help but I was going to make someone pay except, when I returned to Margaret in the next cycle, none of this would have happened.

I'm very good at carrying grudges, even grudges for things that haven't yet occurred.

Chapter 14: Margaret

One evening, about three weeks after the police had been, more visitors came. There were four of them; young, frustrated, barely understandable through the rage that infected them as though it was some kind of disease of the youth.

They shouted at me and kicked my things around. They pushed over my chairs and table and stamped the fire out. They threatened me and swore at me and called me vile names, but all they wanted to know was where the Chinese bitch was. Apparently, they were going to fuck her then fuck her up.

They wouldn't listen when I said she was gone, they just kept saying I must have known where she was because people like us tell each other everything. Their shouting got louder and angrier.

One went into the horsebox and I tried to stop him but he was too strong. He just pushed me aside. I asked him not to damage anything but I could hear him taking his frustrations and anger out on my furniture.

When they were finally sure I had no information, one of them spat on my face and punched me in the stomach. I lay on the ground, gasping for breath as my body tried to cry. I didn't feel afraid; I was just full of sadness and remorse and pain.

Lisa came running up the track. She helped me onto my feet and straightened the outdoor furniture as I leaned against the side of the lorry, still trying to breathe properly. She went inside and came straight out, telling me to go down to her caravan while she tidied up. I told her I wanted to go to bed and she said I could go to bed in her home but I wanted to see what he'd done.

Everything was in a pile in the middle of the lounge, everything from the kitchen, from my sideboard, my cupboards. The mattress had been pulled down from the bed above the cab and he'd urinated on it. My bed linen had been cut with a kitchen knife. The stuffing from the pillows was everywhere. The glass in my photographs was smashed but at least the photographs were still intact.

I leant against the doorframe as I looked at what had been my sanctuary for so many years and I wept.

Lisa said I could stay with her for a week or two while she tidied up and found replacements for everything but I just wanted to sit in my home and cry. She said we should tell Laura because these thugs were going to cause her some damage if they found her. I pulled the phone from my pocket, switched it on, and dialled the number. It went straight to voicemail so I recorded a message and hung up.

Lisa snatched the phone from my hand, redialled the number and left a full account of what had happened. Hearing it from her made it seem so much worse. She named one of the lads and said the ringleader was the son of a senior police officer. She added I was in a bad way, and if I could send some money to replace the things that got broken, that would be good. Lisa can be very forthright when she's riled. She helped me down the lane and put me to bed.

The next day, her whole family went up the track to tidy and clean my home. Lisa made a list of everything that was broken that couldn't be repaired. It was a long list but my memories are more important than the things I own.

I didn't feel very well, so I spent the next week recuperating in Lisa's bed. My bruises came through after a couple of days and I felt stiff and old and useless.

I checked the phone several times. No calls in, no messages back. I was disappointed I'd misjudged Laura so badly.

Chapter 15: Laura

I rolled onto my back and cried. Again. The pain, the dread, the need and despair of not being given the substances my body craved but which would ultimately do it no good anyway. The aching of muscles from the terrible cramps… All these things piled into my consciousness as I cried myself awake again.

Drugs. Can't live with them, can't live without them or, in my case, can't live beyond a year because that's all I get. One year on a loop. Time after time after time.

I'm a couple of thousand and 28 years old because that's how many times I've been through this loop. A couple of thousand loops and I'm actually 28 years old.

I cried with the frustration that comes of starting a new cycle. I cried with loneliness. I cried for the babies I have lost, the husbands and the wives and the boyfriends and girlfriends I could never see again. Well, I could see them again but that wasn't the point.

I cried because the last cycle had ended and it wasn't a bad one. Now, I was in a new cycle and I had things to do and wrongs to right and yet I could barely stand up.

The cold, damp south London air pushed its way through the carpet nailed haphazardly across the window. The squat smelled of damp and of curry from the takeaway shop downstairs.

Yesterday, my lungs had been full of the watery scent of a canal mooring as I toasted my neighbouring boater with a glass of wine for achieving 48 years on the planet. Today, he was 47 once more and about to get cruelly dumped by his girlfriend again.

Today, I had 52 weeks of life in front of me.

I needed to get myself straight. I needed some money, a safe place; I needed to get fit and I needed to focus on not getting sucked back into the world of partying and non-stop music festivals and easy drugs. That had been the first half of the cycle I'd just left.

Do you know how many people die of drug overdoses in the UK every year, or in Europe? Or the world? No, neither do I. All I do know is that I OD and I die but then I don't die.

Year after year, cycle after cycle, I wake up from an overdose which should have killed me except it doesn't. Instead, I wake at the same point exactly one year earlier.

It's like a 'you need to live through this again because someone somewhere likes watching you cry' kind of thing. And I did. I cried my heart out.

Even though I was barely physically functioning, I began to set out my goals for this cycle. I knew I had to feed my brain, give it something to do while my body was dealing with system shock.

I wanted to look into that peculiar money transaction through that private bank in Liechtenstein. I knew the amount, I knew the transfer date, I knew the sending and receiving accounts. What I didn't know was where the money went.

I wanted to spend some time looking into the flight records of an executive jet registered in the Isle of Man.

And I needed to sort Margaret out. I owed her for her kindness and generosity and I owed her for the physical pain and mental anguish she'd been through in the last cycle. There were a couple of things I could do for her but I had to avoid upsetting her. She didn't know me in this cycle but I knew she needed help and I knew she needed it more than she realised. I was probably the only person who could give her what she needed.

A sudden shot of pain through my stomach keeled me over and I dry heaved against the dirty, wooden floor. I wiped my mouth with the back of my hand and lay there, making simple plans. Get fit, get money, get fitter, get into the Nebak compound as a member of staff for Whiteland Security.

Simple.

Getting money was easy. Tomorrow, I was going to buy a lottery ticket. I'd deal with everything else as soon as my body would let me.

Chapter 16: Laura

You can get whatever you want if you know which buttons to push, which levers to pull, which questions to ask and answer. There are some things you can't override - for instance, the amount of time the process needs to take - but you'll still get what you want. You just have to keep your impatience in check.

One week after waking in the squat, I was cleared out and

back in my flat on the farm in the village of Old Weston, Cambridgeshire. I didn't have to go to work yet. I was almost halfway through four weeks of compassionate leave but I needed time to get fit and positioned for the next phase.

I pulled my bike out of the shed and cycled the mile and a half to work. By the time I got to the main security gate at RAF Molesworth, my legs felt like jelly. The USAF airman on the gate gave my pass a brief check, looked scornfully at my bike, raised the barrier and waved me through.

'You look like shit, Laura,' he muttered under his breath as I wobbled in. He was being kind. I looked worse than shit.

RAF Molesworth is not a flying RAF station. It's not even a real RAF station. Out of the full staff, there are two RAF officers on the base and less than two dozen British civilians. The rest of the 500 or so staff are either uniformed USAF personnel or civilian intelligence specialists who work for the CIA, the NSA or the Defence Intelligence Analysis Centre, like me.

Most of the military staff live at nearby RAF Alconbury (also not an RAF station). The majority of the civilians prefer to live off-base and dabble in the culture of a foreign country. I've lived here since I was posted out from the DIAC in Washington DC. I like this place. It's quiet, picturesque and, up to a point, I've been able to work and live my life in an enjoyable bubble of almost solitude.

That point, the point where my life changed, was when my family died in a plane crash. That's why I'm on compassionate leave. When they died, I went off the rails, hit drugs hard, had my OD and that's when I started living in a loop. I figured the time loop thing was related to everything but I had no idea what the connection was.

I've quit my job hundreds of times. I've also just walked away from it hundreds of times. I've travelled all over the world, seen things, seen people and learned things you wouldn't believe. The number one thing I've picked up on is that the best place to garner high value information isn't in the corridors of power or finance or politics. No. To learn the really interesting stuff, you need to go into the shady places where the agents and operators do their cloak and dagger work. Today, I was starting on the path to a shady place I'd visited before.

I used a public computer in the on-base library because nothing says you're serious more than having a US DOD IP address on your communications. I emailed the Whiteland Security recruitment department, asking if they had any vacancies and attached my resumé. I knew the enquiries they'd make and who they'd contact for references.

We'd have a little email chat in the next few days and there would be a couple of Teams calls, but things wouldn't really get moving until they'd vetted me. That would take weeks because the people I work for don't just throw open the doors and offer up information on their high-flying intelligence analysts.

I walked over to the Fitness Centre and booked sessions in the weights, strength and cardiovascular rooms. I really wanted a swimming pool, but the US military doesn't have one in these parts, the best civilian pool is 20 kilometres away in the north of Huntingdon. At this stage of my fitness, a 24-mile round trip on my bicycle with a swim in between would finish me.

I wheeled my bike out past the gate. The same airman gave me a half wave and called me a pussy for walking, but that's

OK. I know all his secrets.

I turned towards the farm, got on the bike and wobbled my way back home.

Chapter 17: Laura

The airport bus pulled up next to the huge Mil Mi-26M helicopter. It was now two months since my enquiry to Whiteland. This was Dubai International Airport but not the smart civilian side where my flight had landed three hours ago.

We unloaded our luggage ourselves and carried it up the tail ramp. The loadmaster checked our names off his clipboard and told us to stow our gear in one of the metal cargo crates.

It was 06.00 local but the air inside the cavernous, heavy lift helicopter was as hot as it had been out on the airport tarmac. My blouse was going to stop looking good in a few minutes. I took a small case out of my jeans pocket and sat on one of the folding seats. The heavyset, mid-30s guy who had followed me up the ramp parked himself next to me, unfolded a golfing magazine and buried his face in it.

47 passengers had transited off the bus. Three of the four large cargo crates were already full, our gear was now loaded into the fourth. It was a light load, not fuel or financially efficient for such a large helicopter. I wondered what it had carried here on the outward journey.

The loadmaster took a microphone from the ramp control panel and I tried to look interested.

‘Welcome aboard, campers. Due to unforeseen circumstances, today’s inflight movie has been cancelled. So has cabin service. If you need the bathroom, there’s a bucket behind the curtain.’ He pointed at the rug hung across the cargo bay. ‘We shall be flying at a height of twenty-five-hundred metres and at a speed of two-hundred thirty kilometres per hour. This cargo hold is not pressurised but you won’t need supplemental oxygen. Flight time will be approximately two and a quarter hours. I’ll be closing the ramp in a moment and we will depart as soon as we have clearance.’

The loadmaster glanced down at his watch before continuing his rehearsed sermon.

‘I’m about to pass a bag round. Please put your mobile phones, tablets, wearable fitness devices, trackers and anything else that has GPS capability inside it. Failure to observe this request will result in a penalty you won’t like. You’ll be able to buy or rent replacement devices at our destination. Details will be in your welcome pack. Thank you for flying with us and I really hope we have a safe journey.’ That got a nervous laugh from a few of us.

I opened the case, took out a pair of ear defenders, plugged them in, leaned back, closed my eyes and tried to sleep.

I was trying really hard when I got nudged in the ribs. The heavyset guy mimed ‘phone’ with his little finger and thumb as he waved the bag at me.

I took the ear defenders out. ‘Don’t have one.’

He looked at me as if I was peculiar.

‘Tablet?’

‘Don’t take them.’

He laughed. ‘So, you got anything for the bag?’

'Nada.'

'Fair enough.' He took the bag back.

I put the plugs back in and closed my eyes. The cargo bay began to vibrate as the two enormous jet engines whiningly started then changed to a deeper pitch as they warmed. Outside, the massive blades slowly began to turn, adding a new vibration to the helicopter. Even at low revs, the cargo bay was a noisy place. I felt sorry for anyone who hadn't brought ear defenders.

Chapter 18: Laura

The corporate HQ of Whiteland Security is in Maryland, USA, just a short drive from the Fort Meade headquarters of the US National Security Agency. It's a well-known building listed on any internet search engine. But the location of the operational HQ of Whiteland is known only in closely guarded circles. Even amongst those who know, it's called Nebak, but it's 200km south of the Saudi Arabian town of the same name. The name is either someone's little joke or a last roll of the subterfuge dice. While the corporate HQ shows up on every modern-day map of Maryland, the Nebak operational HQ doesn't even appear on satellite photographs of Saudi Arabia.

I was dozing when I felt the huge helicopter flare out, lose its forward speed and land with a triple thump of its undercarriage. The pilots kept the engines running so I guessed the bird had somewhere else to get to. The loadmaster was quick on his controls, the ramp opening before I'd even sat upright.

He picked up the microphone and I took my plugs out.

'Thank you for flying Calamity Air. Please take your luggage from the crate and exit the aircraft immediately and I mean yesterday. The bus will take you to the base entrance where you'll be given your ID cards. Don't lose them.'

We emerged, blinking at the harsh desert sunlight. The bus was close to the ramp, engine running. We were driven about 5km to a desert-camo painted building the size of a small aircraft hangar.

Inside, a young woman in desert fatigues sat at a desk. She checked our names against a list, then handed each of us a lanyard with a colour-coded ID card attached. Amongst other information, my ID had my name and photo on the front and a magstripe on the back. I hadn't posed for the photo but I recognised the clothes as an outfit I'd worn during the second Teams recruitment call.

When we had all been marked off the list and handed our passes, she stood behind her desk and pressed a button which opened the wall behind her.

'This elevator will take you down to the accommodation level. Your room number is on your ID. Inside your rooms, you'll find a welcome pack and your induction itinerary.'

The elevator was a large freight lift but it still took two runs to get all 47 of us down to the accommodation level. I was in the second wave, pressed up against the heavyset guy's chest and sandbagged from behind by someone's suitcase.

'Do we need an introduction?' he asked.

'If you don't make your hard-on go away, I'll give you one you'll never forget.'

'That's my wallet.'

'It's not a very big one.'

'My ex-wife said the same.'

A couple of the passengers snorted, someone giggled, but nobody else felt the need to talk.

The elevator stopped and we squeezed out into a corridor wide enough to drive a couple of SUVs through side by side. I shouldered my kitbag and glanced at my ID. My accommodation was Blue 51. The sign opposite the elevator signposted directions for Yellow, Green, Blue and Purple. I headed to Blue.

'Can I give you a hand with that?'

'So, not content with interfering with me in the elevator, you're now stalking me to see where I live?'

'Aww, no. I know where you live, I looked at your ID. I'm just offering to help with your bag.'

'Where are you going?'

'Blue twenty-four.'

'Are you going to follow me around all the time?' I asked.

'You're not that cute.'

'Neither are you.'

'My ex-wife used to say that too.'

'I don't need help. Let's just head out,' I said.

'Whatever you say.'

We joined the dozen or so other people who were moving in the direction of Blue.

'Did you order the enhanced room service?' he asked as we walked.

'Are you base comedian?'

'No, I just like enhanced room service.'

I grunted up at him as we turned a corner into a corridor that had a thick blue line painted down the middle of the floor. We started losing people as their room numbers came up. We walked on a short way until we got to Blue 24.

'Well, this is where I get off. Don't forget to write, honey.'

I shook my head like I was unimpressed at his attempt at humour. He swiped his ID card down the reader and peeled off into his room.

I walked on until I got to Blue 51, swiped my card, opened the door and walked into a wall of air conditioning.

Chapter 19: Laura

I knew the contents of the induction pack already but I sat on the bed and leafed through it. My induction was scheduled to start in an hour. I unpacked a fresh outfit, had a shower, got dressed, picked up the induction pack and walked to the induction room.

The thickset guy fell in alongside me as I walked down the corridor.

'Have you checked out the TV stations we can get?' he asked.

'No.'

'Seen the catalogue of books in the library?' he tried.

'No.'

'How about the equipment rooms in the gym?'

'No,' I said.

'Have you even read the induction pack?'

'Yes.'

'What's the fifth word in the second sentence on page twenty-five?'

‘Relationships,’ I said as I pressed the button to call the elevator.

He flicked open his induction pack and counted quietly.

‘I believe it is. How did you know?’

‘Because I’ve read the induction pack.’

The elevator doors opened.

‘And memorised it?’ he asked. ‘Is that your thing? A party trick?’

Two other people joined us in the elevator.

‘I don’t do party tricks,’ I said, trying not to smile.

We travelled to the next floor in silence. The induction room had chairs along three sides of a square with a white-board/markerboard on the fourth side. The four of us from the elevator joined three others already seated. A tall woman in her late 40s seated in front of the markerboard stood as the door closed behind us.

‘Take a seat and we’ll get started. I hope you all had a pleasant journey?’

There was a mixed grumble of yesses.

‘Good to know. Today is familiarisation day. Your time will be spent on this induction, the contents of your packs and you’ll get an introductory walkaround. Tomorrow, you’re all on duty in your respective sections. You’ll find the details of your workaround and duty information on the last page of your packs.’

A couple of people flicked their packs open.

‘These are the inflexible rules. This is a civilian outfit run on military lines. You’re all former military so you’ll be familiar with the culture. You’re on a six-month tour of duty which may be extended if we like each other. You are being very well paid and you get to live in comfortable accommodation free of charge. You will not drink while you are here. This also applies to drugs.'

Her gaze briefly landed on me but she didn't skip a beat.

'You do not smoke on duty or in your quarters. Smoking is confined to the smoking rooms on each floor. If you are required to work outside, you will receive a safety and security briefing in the armoury; details in your induction packs. You will work under the direct supervision of a product lead. Product leads own every operational aspect of this facility. They're a bit like sergeants in the military because we all know the military wouldn't function if it wasn't for the sergeants, don't we?'

There was another chorus of yesses.

'You will be assigned a place on a duty roster by your product lead. They will check you out on your duties but you have been recruited for a specific role that we know you can do. Are these things clear?'

More yesses.

'That's about all I have for you. Everything else you need to know is in your induction packs, including your reporting lines and your product leaders. At the end of your six-month tour, you will either revert to normal civilian life or take a three-week break before coming back for a second tour. Anyway, just in case you have any questions which you haven't asked because you're intimidated by my winning personality, you can find my contact details inside the packs. However, you can also use the Intranet to search for information. It's accessible through the TVs in your rooms. If you want to rent or buy tablets, laptops or phones, please see the quartermaster whose details you will find where?' She waited for someone to pipe up.

‘In the packs or on the Intranet,’ said the redhead.

‘My name is Mary Havers and my work here is done. Thank you.’

Thickset guy turned to me and said, ‘Page five, second paragraph. Third sentence. Second word?’

‘Date.’

‘Well, that’s kinda pushy but alright. Tonight?’

Chapter 20: Laura

I grade all aircraft landings. At the low end of the scale are the landings you can barely walk away from. Perhaps the aircraft came in sideways and wobbled down the tarmac on fewer than the correct number of wheels or maybe it banged the runway so hard you thought one or more of the tyres might burst. In the middle of the scale are the hard-ish landings, the ones which would spill your drink if you were allowed to have a drink just before thumpdown. At the top end of the scale are the soft as a feather landings.

Very few landings score above seven because I’m a tough judge.

Emirates flight EK770 was an easy nine on the landing scale. The Boeing 777 executed a beautifully judged touch-down with no last-minute changes of pace, no sudden shifts of altitude; the aircraft almost kissed the Cape Town tarmac.

Passport control showed interest in the six months I’d spent in Dubai, the journey to Saudi Arabia, down to Nebak and back to Dubai never appearing on anybody’s documentation. They wanted to know how long I was planning to be in South Africa. Customs gave me a hard stare when I walked through the green channel with just my kitbag but I knew they would have x-rayed it, sniffed it and labelled it as no risk before it even hit the luggage carousel.

The taxi dropped me outside the hotel in the affluent suburb of Constantia, 15km south of the centre of Cape Town.

The concierge didn't sneer at my lack of beautifully matched luggage, and didn't freak out at me rocking up in scruffy jeans and a crumpled t-shirt an hour before midnight, so I gave him a generous tip and a dirty smile. I checked in, went up to the suite, showered and hit the sack.

The next morning, I ate breakfast on the balcony. The sun was breaking through light cloud and starting to heat the crisp, clear air. Birds called to each other from the trees and bushes. Below me, the swimming pool beckoned seductively.

I felt overloaded. This much sensory input was a lightyear away from the airconditioned underground drabness of a six-month tour in Nebak.

I promised myself I would give the pool some action later.

I sipped my coffee and mentally checked my plan. Over the last couple of months, the enquiries I'd put into the field for Margaret had brought back three solid leads and one that felt flaky. I knew I would have to go back to the UK to see Margaret, even though she hadn't met me yet, but it looked like I needed to go and see someone else while I was there. They were going to help me tie down the flaky lead. Everything felt good.

I leaned back in my chair and stretched as if I was a plant reaching for the sun's rays.

'You make that wrap look good but you look even better

out of it.'

I straightened out of my stretch, sat up and turned towards the doorway.

'I thought you were never going to get out of bed.'

'You know it's six AM by my body clock?' said the thickset man.

'Same by mine but look at the day we have.' I gestured at the world in front of us. 'Are you going to waste all this?'

'I have to catch up on my sleep. I didn't get here until two AM and you didn't let me get much rest.'

'Oliver, we spent the last six months flirting. That's serious foreplay. I've got itches that need to be scratched. Sleep isn't even on the plan.'

'The no-frat clause in the contract really got to you, huh?'

'Six months of you badgering me didn't make keeping a lid on things easy.'

'I always had my mind on the job.'

'Yeah, right.'

'So, if sleep isn't on the plan, what is? And why are we in South Africa?'

'A little sightseeing, a walk, a drive. Some pool but not the kind I beat you at every time. Eating out, early nights, early mornings. Relax.'

'You had me until early mornings.'

'Stay in bed then but it's the best part of the day and I'm not going to miss a minute.'

'We could do those things anywhere. Why South Africa?'

'I haven't been down this way for a while. I thought it would make a nice change.' And I'm looking for someone who can make someone else's life a little better, but I left those words unsaid.

Chapter 21: Laura

'Wow!' he said as we rounded Chapman's Peak Drive. 'That's some view!'

And 'wow' it was. The stunning Noordhoek Beach spread out below us like a piece of paradise. The view from the top of the rise was the kind of view Hollywood likes to show you, the kind of view directors scour the earth for.

We drove into the pull-in and left the hire car in the car park. The hotel had given us a hamper with a light lunch and a couple of beach towels. We nodded to the security guards and headed down the boardwalk towards the water's edge. Oliver reached out and held my hand.

'Do you want the waves crashing onto the rocks or the waves lapping at the white sand 'cos this beach gives us both?' he asked.

'Head over towards the shipwreck, maybe do some snorkelling?'

'Snorkelling? Is that a euphemism?'

I punched him in the arm. 'You've got a dirty mind.'

'You complaining?'

'Not yet,' I admitted.

'OK then. Let's set up on the edge of the dunes then go get ourselves wet.'

'Is *that* a euphemism?' I asked.

'You know, I'm beginning to wonder which one of us has the dirty mind.'

'It's you,' I said. 'Don't make this thing harder than it needs to be.' I laughed and ran to the dunes while he stood there, holding the hamper, mouth open.

We settled down on the southern curve of the beach.

sheltered from the occasionally gusty wind by dunes of sand and tufty grass. We walked in the direction of what's left of the shipwreck 'Kakapo' which beached in 1900. We paddled in the sea up to our ankles.

'The water's so cold it's almost painful.'

'We could rent a couple of suits, if you want to go swimming? Or diving?' I offered.

'Yeah, I don't know. This beach is fantastic but the pool by the hotel is more me.'

'OK.'

I looked back up the beach. I reckoned it was 3 kilometres from here to the pavilion.

'I'm going to run from there and back to the dunes. Coming?'

He turned and looked up the beach.

'Nooo, you knock yourself out. I'll take a slow walk back to the picnic and start unpacking.'

'You're a pussy!' I called as I started my run.

I kept to the water's edge where the wet sand was firm beneath my feet. I covered the distance to the pavilion in 10 minutes which, for me, is a sloppy time. I tried to knock 30 seconds off that on the return, but the sand towards the dunes was dry and deep and slowed me down, so I eased off and jogged back at a comfortable pace.

There were three of them. Oliver was on his back with a knife at his throat. They were young, maybe 21, and they all had knives. Two of them looked uncomfortable and none looked like they did this kind of thing for a living. Not one of them looked like they'd be any opposition in a fight.

The guy in the blue shirt, standing back from Oliver, he needed to go down first. I could see the guy with a knife to

Oliver's throat was on the cusp of making a fatal mistake, and I didn't want him to die here.

I took heaving lungfuls of air, pretending the run had been hard work.

'Hello, lady,' said the one in the red shorts. 'Won't you tell your friend here he needs to give us his watch and his wallet?'

I took a couple of breaths before I answered. 'We don't want any trouble. Why don't you leave us alone and then nobody gets hurt?'

He laughed. Red shorts had a nice voice and a cultured accent. He wasn't just in the wrong place at the wrong time, he was doing the wrong job and he was doing it badly.

'We will leave just as soon as we have been paid. This part of the beach is ours and there is a fee for being here.'

I didn't want any of them to get seriously hurt, but the guy at Oliver's throat was about to die and only Oliver and I knew it.

'I've got twenty dollars. American. You can have that if you just go away.'

'I like your style, so what we'll do is take your twenty dollars and your man's watch and wallet, and then you can stay here for the rest of the day.'

I slipped my left hand into the pocket of my shorts and held out two ten-dollar bills. Red shorts ambled towards me. As he reached out, I dropped to a knee, punched him in the testicles, punched him in the face with a left-handed uppercut, picked up the knife he'd dropped and threw it at the boy who was holding the knife to Oliver's throat. The handle struck him between his eyes. He dropped his knife and rolled over, dazed and shocked. Oliver swept up the knife, scrambled over his attacker and flattened the lad in the blue shirt.

In less than a couple of seconds everything had changed. Red shorts was down, retching and bleeding, blue shirt was on his knees, Oliver holding one of his arms up behind his back, and the throat knifeman was still dazed and on his back.

I rolled red shorts over and helped him onto his knees. He swayed unsteadily, blood flowing from his nose and mouth.

'What's your name?' I asked.

'Jmsh.'

'James?'

'Yethsh.'

'Keep the money, James, but maybe get a different job because you're shit at this one.'

He shook his head, blood dripping from his face onto the sand.

'Theresh no jobsh,' he said quietly, through his damaged face.

'Where do you live, James?'

He looked up at me, not happy I was asking this question.

'DeeGeePee.'

'Da Gamma Park?' I asked.

He nodded but didn't like I knew what DGP stood for.

'You're a long way from home.'

He didn't answer so I looked around. Blue shirt was still immobilised by Oliver and throat guy looked so dazed I doubted he knew his own name.

'What do you want to do now?' I asked Oliver.

He shrugged. 'Still waiting for that picnic.'

'Yeah, good call. I'm famished.' I turned to James. 'We're

going to pack up in an hour and we'll be gone for the day but if I see you or your gang on this beach again, James, I'm going to do much worse than kick your backside in front of your friends. Do you get me?'

He nodded; blood dripped down onto his front.

'Let him go,' I said to Oliver.

'You sure? We could take them to the security guards in the car park.'

'Let them all go. If James or his gang come here again, I'll break lots of bones. Do you hear me, James? Lots of bones.'

He nodded sullenly but his expression said he got the message. Oliver turned blue shirt loose. He went straight to throat guy, helped him to his feet and, together, they helped James stand. Something fluttered onto the sand as he turned to go.

'Be safe, James,' I said. 'I'll be watching for you.'

The three of them left the dunes and headed northwards, away from the beach. I picked up the debit card that had fallen out of James' pocket, looked at it and put it in my pocket.

Oliver brushed sand off the top of the picnic hamper and opened it.

'If that's the starter, I can't wait for the main course!'

'The main course is later, back at the hotel. That was just a snack to tide us over.'

He looked up from unpacking. 'Am I going to like the main course?'

'I think so. I'm going to put you in the middle of the bed and ride you until my muscles give out.'

'Oh… I think I'm going to enjoy that.'

Chapter 22: Laura

The next day, by mutual agreement, I drove. I'd told Oliver we were going sightseeing but that was all I told him. When the mountain road became a dirt track, he grumbled almost quietly and I knew he was complaining about my driving.

'You're very snarky this morning, dear,' I patronised.

'I'm short of sleep, I have bruises and you're throwing this car all over the track.'

'I'm trying to avoid the potholes my navigator isn't telling me about,' I said.

'You kept your navigator awake half the night and you're the reason I have bruises.'

'I have bruises too but mine are mostly internal.'

He sniggered like a child.

'Keep going,' he said.

'Alright then. You're definitely not a morning person-'

'No. I meant keep going on this track, not keep going telling me my bad points.'

I smiled and said, 'Oh. OK.'

'But you can tell me why we're driving up a mountain track at this ungodly hour, if you like?'

'We're going to see someone - or something, maybe both - and nine am is not an ungodly hour.'

'It is when you woke me at three and didn't let me sleep until gone six.'

'You're soft,' I said.

'Not all the time.'

I chuckled and said, 'No, you're not soft all the time. How much further?'

'According to the map, we take the next right but it's

looking patchy from there.'

'I'll take the next right and keep going until we get to the end.'

'This map doesn't show an end,' he said.

'Where's the next right?'

'I have no idea. This map isn't much good.'

We almost missed it, the open gateway behind a tin-roofed barn and the even more dirt-tracked dirt track that wound higher into the mountains. The faded, wooden sign said '*Cape Heartland Wine Estate*' in what was once fine script below a regal-looking crown. The dirt track was held together by potholes so I slowed down and drove carefully.

Five kilometres later, we pulled up outside a modern, L-shaped bungalow with an immaculate swimming pool to the side.

'Nice place!'

'A little out of the way,' I replied.

'Off the beaten track and then some. Do you think it's deliberate, the drive up here being so hard?'

Before I could answer, the front door opened and a young woman stepped out. She wore a simple shift dress and gold sandals. She looked tanned, lean, fit and in better shape than most other mid 20-year-olds.

'Kan ek jou help?' she asked in a thick Afrikaans accent.

'Ons soek Johannes Marula, is hy hier?' I asked.

'He's not here today,' she continued in Afrikaans. 'I'm his daughter. Can I ask what you want?'

'I'm visiting from England and I've got a message for him from an old friend; they used to hang around together.'

She looked puzzled. 'I didn't know Dad knew anyone over there but you can't speak to him right now. He's the other side of the Cape at a conference. He won't be back until the day after tomorrow. Can I give him a message for you when he calls in?'

I needed her to feel relaxed so I gave her a harmless message that would get him curious.

'He wouldn't know me but could you tell him that Laura Todd from Hereford, England is in Cape Town until the end of next week and I have a message from an old friend of his?'

'Sure, I can do that. Where are you staying?'

I gave her the name of the hotel and she looked impressed.

'Dad will probably come straight back here. Do you have a number he can call?'

'He can reach me through the hotel but I'd like to see him. I don't mind driving up here again.'

'I'll tell him,' she said as she held out her hand. 'Nala.'

'Laura,' I said as I shook hands with her. 'And this is Oliver.' She flashed a brief smile at him then turned back towards the house.

We were almost at the bottom of the bumpy track when Oliver spoke. 'Gonna tell me what that was about?'

'Delivering a message.'

'I don't speak Afrikaans but my Dutch is good enough to get that you're delivering a message from Hereford, England.'

'Yes.'

'And I caught you told her your surname was Todd?'

'I did, yes.'

He pursed his lips but didn't speak again until we reached the hotel.

Chapter 23: The Old Man

He was glad to be on his way home. Three nights in a chain hotel, even the most expensive chain in South Africa, was more than enough for him. He disliked hotels and expensive ones attracted the kind of people he didn't like. Flashy people, people with no taste or class, loud and brash people. He preferred the quiet comfort and familiarity of his own home.

He checked out at 7am, loaded his truck before driving from the hotel and away from the coast, heading inland for the R63 highway in the mountains. The N1 highway would have been a more direct, shorter route but he didn't like the coastal towns and cities it passed through. They were glitzy, touristy and… not authentic. Too much of South Africa had sacrificed the real character of the country while chasing the Tourist Rand and he didn't like that.

Once he had crossed the Western Cape border, he pulled into a layby for lunch. The roadside foodshack looked safe but, out of habit, he checked his 9mm Vektor semi-automatic pistol, slid it back into its belt holster in the small of his back, his windcheater on, and stepped out into the humid air. He bought a Boerie roll and a bowl of salad then sat on a wicker chair under a tattered umbrella to enjoy the dishes. He handed the bowls back to the vendor, wiped his hands on his trousers and bought a bottle of Sparletta before getting back into his truck to continue along the blacktop towards Cape Town.

Two hours from his destination, he pulled over for a toilet break, to stretch his legs and ease his aching back. He leaned against the side of the truck and made mental notes of the things he needed to do when he got home. The conference hadn't been a complete waste of time and it was always good to network but the local wine market felt saturated, though the wine producers who were selling abroad seemed to be making good money.

The EU and Australian markets were difficult to crack but he was going to look at trying to sell overseas. South Africa had strong trade links with Russia and he hoped he'd be able to piggy-back off of those. He'd ask Nala to use the Internet to research this. He didn't use the Internet much; he didn't trust a place where so much information just seemed to be accessible.

He pulled a large, ancient mobile phone from his pocket and called home.

He drove the rest of the way in a distracted state. Laura Todd? From Hereford, England? Years ago, when he'd lived there, he had known Margaret Todd. Was Laura Todd a relative? From Nala's description she was too young to be a daughter so a granddaughter, perhaps? Who was she? How the hell did she track him down and what did she want?

He would have to make a call when he got home.

Chapter 24: Laura

'You didn't have to come,' I said.

He grumbled under his breath.

'Really,' I added. 'You could have stayed in the hotel and made eyes at the barmaid by the pool.'

He quietly grumbled some more.

I went on, 'She wouldn't have enjoyed, it but you could have made her a *little* bit miserable instead of sitting in the car making me a *lot* more miserable.'

'I wanted to come but did we have to leave so early?'

'You saw the message. He wants to see me at eight, so here we are, about to hit every pothole in this bumpy road, nice and early.'

He grumbled again. I could see his lips moving but couldn't hear him.

'You're enjoying this,' I said.

'I haven't had so much fun this early in the morning since I got my divorce in the post.'

'I like that you're comparing me to a divorce. That's a new level of flattering.'

'Not you,' he said. 'This.' He waved a hand at the mountainous countryside as we bumped our way up the track.

'I'll make it up to you. When we get back to the hotel, we can go for a swim and then you can take me to bed and show me a different kind of bumping.'

He slid me a glance to see if I meant it. He saw I did and his face burst into a childish grin.

'Well, it would be rude not to take you up on the offer.'

'I was hoping you would take me up on the offer and then we could be rude.'

'You're exactly the kind of girl I should have met ten years ago.'

'Pervert,' I said. 'Ten years ago, I was eighteen.' Except, that wasn't true because, ten years ago, I was still a couple of thousand and 28 years old.

We lapsed into one of our silences for the rest of the journey. He was probably thinking about what his life could have looked like if he'd made different decisions. I was thinking about what I was going to say at the end of this journey and how I was going to say it.

We pulled up in front of the bungalow again but, unlike our last visit, nobody came to meet us. We got out and looked around.

'Want to check out the pool?' I asked.

'Didn't bring my trunks.'

'Maybe Nala could lend you something?' I suggested as we walked toward the front door.

'I don't think I would fit into anything of hers.'

'You'd like the chance to try.'

'You, lady, have a really dirty mind.'

'It's one of my best qualities,' I admitted.

I pushed the button and an angry dog barked inside. Oliver raised an eyebrow.

'Big dog,' I said.

'Awww, thanks.'

'Not you.'

'I know and it's not a cuddly, little fellow like me, either.'

Before I could reply, the door opened and it wasn't Nala. He was about the same age as Margaret but where she was short, pale and soft-skinned, he was tall, tanned and leathery.

I broke the ice.

'Johannes Marula?'

'Ja, dis ek?' His accent had a Cape Town twang.

I explained that Oliver didn't speak much Afrikaans and asked if we could talk in English. He said we could but didn't invite us in.

'As I told Nala, I have a message for you from someone you

knew in Hereford, England.'

'Someone I knew who now lives in Hereford? Who would that be?'

'Margaret Todd.'

He looked blank.

'I don't know anyone by that name,' he said. 'Did she live in Cape Town under a different name before she moved over there?'

I felt uncomfortable having this conversation out in the open but I could see he wasn't going to let us in.

'You looked after her financial affairs when you worked in Hereford. You also had a relationship with her.'

He looked puzzled for a moment then switched to outraged.

'And your name's Todd too? Is this some kind of a shake-down? Are you trying to blackmail me? I've never even been to England. I've never even left South Africa!' His pitch became strident as he got more agitated. He went on. 'I think, whoever you are, you'd better leave before I call the authorities!'

He stepped back, not to close the door but to allow the large, well-built man who came from further inside to get close. He looked interesting but the pump-action shotgun that was pointed at my stomach interested me more. The trouble with pump-action shotguns in rural places like this is that people tend to use them. I tried to keep talking but I caught a glimpse of Oliver leaning slowly towards the doorframe.

'Look, we don't need to create a scene here,' I said. 'Your real name is John, isn't it, Johannes?'

'Get off my property or I'll have you shot.'

'I'd rather not be shot either way, John. Can we talk about this?'

'My name isn't John and you have precisely five seconds to get back in your car and go before something terrible happens to you both.'

Although he was talking to me, he hadn't discounted Oliver. He wasn't blind and he wasn't stupid. I tried one last time.

'Do you have a lawyer in town, John? Somewhere we can meet for a civilised discussion without you pointing a gun at us?'

'Just get off my property. I'm counting to five. One.'

'Alright, John. We're going. Your daughter knows where to reach me. We need to talk before things get really serious.'

'Two.'

'Let's go,' I said to Oliver who straightened up from leaning against the doorpost and followed me back to the car.

'Three,' he shouted.

I started the car and pulled slowly away from the bungalow, back onto the bumpy track.

'You know, Princess, for what was an eight o'clock meeting with some guy in a winery, that was an eye-opener. Are all your meetings as exciting as that?'

'You weren't excited,' I said. 'I saw you lean into the doorpost. That's a classic move to split the targets and get out of the direct line of fire.'

'True but I only use that tactic in *really* exciting meetings. You want to tell me what this is all about? Because someone pointing a Remmington Eight-Seventy Fieldmaster in my direction isn't what I got out of bed for.'

'I guess I owe you that. Back to the hotel for a swim,

shower, a little chat and maybe some after-chat sex?'

'I'm going to be cool and laid back about this and agree to that whole timetable. You're going to be cool and laid back and not hold out in the discussion.'

Chapter 25: Laura

After lunch, we moved from the dining room to our suite, sat on the balcony with our drinks and I told him the story behind our visit to the winery.

'So… you're telling me you were thinking this guy who has been living in South Africa under a false identify for decades would just go along with whatever you wanted?'

'I wasn't expecting him to bring a gun to a word fight.'

'A Remmington pump-action isn't a big gun, Laura, but it's bigger than a bunch of words.'

'I could have taken care of both of them and you know what I mean.'

'Maybe I do, maybe I don't. What about the others? Because there will be others. What are you going to do about them?'

'I figure that maybe one or two of the people he bribed for his false identity could still be alive but they're probably not working any more. Retired, most likely.'

'Retired, dishonest people are the worst kind. They'll fight like hell to keep their pension and stay out of jail.'

'I know,' I said. 'But they won't need to fight. I have a gift for them.'

'How are you going to get close enough to give them this magic gift?'

'I'm just going to use my charm and my talent... And I'll smile sweetly at them.'

'OK, so you've got a plan and you've got a bunch of information. You can put it all together and two plus two equals four. That's nice. What kind of timescale are you looking at?'

'I want to be out of South Africa by the end of next week, like we planned.'

We paused the conversation to watch the two vans pull up the drive and stop in front of reception. Doors opened and closed as three people got out of each van.

'You know, I am headed back to Michigan. Would you like to come back with me?'

'Mmmm... That's tempting but I have to go back to the UK to see some old friends. I'd be cool with coming over afterwards?'

'Now that is a nice idea. Do you think the cops would mind if I ordered another coffee before they arrest us?'

'I'm pretty sure they wouldn't care, Oliver.'

'I was just getting really comfortable and could do with another.'

The telephone beside the bed rang. I got up, went inside to answer it then walked back to the balcony.

'Reception just said we have some visitors on their way up.'

'Which way is this going to go?' he asked.

'They'll either take us away in their vans and we'll be questioned somewhere or they're going to take us away in their vans and we'll be *questioned* somewhere.'

He slumped his head forward in mock defeat.

I turned to answer the respectful knock at the door. The spyglass showed me four people in civilian clothes but with South African Police Service stab-vests over the top.

I unlocked the door and stepped back to hold it wide open for them.

'Come in, officers.'

They did. The room seemed a lot smaller with five of us in it.

'You are Laura Guerra?'

'I am.'

'And is Oliver Jago with you?'

'I'm out here,' he called from the balcony.

'We have warrants for your arrest. Can you please accompany us to our vehicles outside?'

I didn't move.

'Who is 'we'?' I asked.

'We are the South African Police Service,' he said, flashing an impressive badge with an ID card beside it.

'No, you misunderstand me. Which department?'

'I am Detective Sergeant Mbebe of the Crime Combating and Investigation Division, Madam.'

I couldn't remember the last time I was called madam and it made me smile. Oliver walked in from the balcony.

'I'm pleased you found something to smile about, Princess,' he said.

'The Crime Combating and Investigation Division want to take us away for questioning. They have warrants for our arrest, apparently.'

'What do the warrants say we've done?' Oliver asked.

'I haven't seen them yet.' I turned towards the sergeant who was clearly not expecting to lose control of this whole show.

'Can we see the warrants please?' I asked.

'We will share those with you down at the station,' he said.

I looked around. The other three were beginning to look off-balance too.

'I would like you to make a call before we go,' I said.

'You can make your one call from the station.'

This was getting repetitive so I made a move to end this farce.

'No, sergeant,' I said firmly. 'You misunderstand me. I would like you to take out your mobile phone and make one call before we move from this room.'

He looked surprised and affronted by my order, an order from someone he'd been told to pick up.

'Who would you like me to call?'

'I would like you to call the National Intelligence Agency in Musanda, Pretoria. I have the number here, if you don't.'

Now he looked really off-balance.

'We can call them from the station,' he repeated.

'When you get through to the duty desk, please ask for the director and tell his PA that Laura Guerra is calling. Or you can try the director at home. I have that number too, if you don't?'

The other three started shuffling uneasily at the change in dynamics. Rightly so. Although the NIA is not part of the Police Service command, the director's boss - the Director General of the NIA - answers only to the President of South Africa.

I was suddenly a whole new threat and the sergeant knew he was out of position and out of his depth.

'Wait here, please,' he said and stepped out of the room. The three remaining officers looked a lot more uncomfortable but stayed put.

'Anyone want some coffee?' asked Oliver as he picked up

the phone to call room service.

Chapter 26: Laura

'What happens now?' he asked.

'Now? I'm thinking I'd like to hit the pool for another swim. How 'bout you?'

'Well, this is the after-discussion sex, yes?'

'Yes. Well, it was. Unless you can saddle up again?'

'Jesus, don't you ever let up?'

'You shouldn't be so talented,' I said.

'You're hyperactive in every department, you know that? You think quicker than a computer, you eat more than a horse and, for a short p-'

'I prefer economically packaged,' I interrupted.

'Wow! For an economically packaged person, you're hard. Really hard.'

'Are you still mad at me because of the beach?'

'What?' he asked, visibly surprised.

'The boy with the knife at your neck,' I said. 'You were about to kill him.'

'I was?' He gave me a flat look.

'Ollie, I can recognise a wrist-block. You were about half a twist away from breaking his wrist, turning the knife upwards and slamming his face down onto the blade. Are you mad at me because I changed the playing field?'

He didn't say anything for five beats, he just looked up at me as I sat astride him. Then, he pulled me down until we were face-to-face.

‘You called me Ollie,’ he said softly. ‘You have never called me Ollie before. Only my mom called me Ollie and, even then, she only called me Ollie when I was exceptionally good.’

I licked the end of his nose and he recoiled.

‘Was that often?’ I asked.

‘Being exceptionally good, you mean?’

‘Yes.’

‘Not often, no.’

I wiggled around a little.

‘I need to either sit up and get off you or we need to go again.’

He pushed me over onto my back and I wrapped my legs around his hips.

‘And pushy. You’re exceptionally pushy.’ He leant down and kissed me. ‘But a man’s gotta do what a man’s gotta do.’

He slid off me and headed for the bathroom.

After a while, I heard the shower running. It wasn’t long before he came back, showered and wearing a towel around his waist.

He stood in front of the full-length mirror and combed out the shower tangles from his thick, dark hair. He looked at me in the mirror.

‘When I asked ‘what happens now’, I was thinking about the guy up at the winery and the South African Police Service.’

‘The SAPS will have an internal investigation to find out how a team of detectives were sent on a wild goose chase with blank pro-forma warrants that hadn’t been signed off. They’ll find someone on the staff who they’ll scapegoat. Whoever that is will take early retirement. The person who *actually* ordered for us to be brought in will stay hidden, but my contact in the NIA could probably get a name for us in a day or two.'

'And that's another thing: Wasn't it convenient that you opened up that line of communication with the Director of the NIA from Nebak a couple of months ago?'

'Wasn't it?'

'And it was so lucky that you told him we'd be visiting Johannes what's-his-name to check an old corruption allegation. You used operational credentials for the chat with the NIA Director and you called him over the Pentagon network for extra buy-in?'

'So very lucky.'

He turned to face me.

'You are either the most incredibly gifted mission planner I've ever met or you're a witch.'

I said nothing. He moved to the wardrobe and slipped on a clean shirt while I watched his muscles at work.

'I could be both,' I said.

'Are you?'

'No. I think I met a witch last year, though.'

'A real one or one of those twenty-first century, new age, hippy types?'

'Ooh, that was disparaging. Anyway, I think she was a real one. I didn't get to know her long enough but she could read.'

'Tea leaves?'

I thought back to Margaret in her lorry on the ancient road in Wiltshire.

'She read the fields and the clouds. And the animals. And the flowers. And insects. It's like she is connected to them.'

'Yeah,' he said. 'A couple of hundred years ago, that would

definitely have gotten her burned at the stake.'

I watched him pull on clean shorts and trousers.

'Are you going to lie there all evening or are you going to get dressed for dinner?'

'I was just thinking it's been quite a day.'

'It has been. Now, get dressed, please. I need to feed the inner man.'

I slipped out of bed and headed for the bathroom.

Chapter 27: Laura

By arrangement, we arrived back at the winery at noon two days later. The door didn't open when we pulled up outside the bungalow.

I pressed the doorbell and we heard the big dog barking before Nala's father opened the door and greeted us curtly.

'Miss Todd. Or Miss Guerra. Whatever your real name is.'

I decided to play it his way.

'John. Or Johannes. Whatever your real name is but we both know what your name really is, don't we, John?'

'I won't invite you in. I understand I have to see you but you're not welcome.'

'OK,' I said. 'We won't be long anyway. I'm going to tell you what I want. You can sleep on it for twenty-four hours while you try to figure out how not to give it to me and then I'll come back so we can sign the agreement. After that, I leave South Africa and you never see me again if you stick to the contract.'

His body language was defensive but I could see his mind

working behind his eyes.

'What do you want?'

'You will give ten percent of the ownership of the winery to Margaret Todd.'

He spluttered and, even under his leathery skin, I could see he was turning pink with rage.

I continued, 'And, on the first day of every month, you will send Margaret five percent of the winery's turnover. Yes, I mean turnover, John. That's five percent of the turnover for the previous month.'

'Whaaaat?' His voice rose to a shriek so high-pitched it didn't seem possible to have come from him.

'And there's a penalty clause in the agreement. An incentive clause, if you prefer. Failure to meet the monthly deadline will increase the amount outstanding by an additional ten percent a day for each day the deadline is not met.'

He could barely find words so I wanted to make sure he understood how quickly this change was coming at him.

'I will have this agreement delivered to the winery's email address later today. You'll need to get it checked out with your legal people. I appreciate solicitors work at their own pace so I'll allow five days for that. This means, John, that, in six days, the agreement will be live and I'll leave South Africa next week. On the first of next month, you'll pay five percent of this month's turnover and transfer ten percent of the ownership to Margaret Todd. Am I clear?'

I stopped speaking and looked at him. He found his voice.

'You might have friends in unexpectedly high places but this is robbery!'

'No, John. Leaving a recently widowed woman with no money, having swindled everything from her possession?

That's robbery. This is just a small act of penitence but, if you want to talk about what is robbery and what isn't, I'm prepared to put all of the information I have in the hands of the public prosecutor. Then, you really would lose everything, including the right to live in South Africa.'

He wasn't seeing it my way.

'Robbery,' he said firmly.

'Stealing all of Margaret Todd's money wasn't robbery?'

'That was… It didn't happen like that. She gave it to me. It was a present. A gift.'

'John the Bastard. That's how she named you when we discussed this. She was right. You're a proper bastard and a thief. Anyway, these are the terms. You either agree to them or I go public with everything I have.' I turned to Oliver. 'We're done here, let's go. I need a shower, I feel contaminated.'

Chapter 28: Laura

We were cooking in the mid-afternoon South African sun. Factor 50, swimming costumes, a good book and the remains of a fish salad on the plates on the poolside table.

I turned onto my stomach and squinted into the shadow cast by the giant sunshade. Oliver sat in the gloom, his deckchair facing me. His head was tilted back, eyes closed and he was breathing deeply. I studied him; slightly too-long hair, an open face, broad shoulders and a deep, wide chest. They were features I had come to know so well in a short time but it's never a bad thing to take in something you appreciate, is it?

'What?'

‘Nothing,’ I said.

‘You’re staring.’

‘You have your eyes shut,’ I complained.

‘I can feel your stare. It feels like I’m being studied.’

‘Yes,’ I agreed. ‘You are.’

‘Why?’

‘I’m making memories.’

He opened one eye and peered at me.

‘Good ones?’

‘This one goes down in the plus column.’

‘Well, that’s reassuring.’

He closed his eye and we didn’t speak for a couple of minutes.

‘This is one of the strangest holidays I’ve had.’

‘Only one of the strangest?’ I asked.

He dodged the question.

‘I don’t want this to go to your head but you don’t seem fazed by anything unexpected and that makes me consider this question: Is this routine for you? This is a normal kind of holiday?’

‘There’s less combat in this one than a normal kind of holiday.’

Both his eyes flicked open and he gave me a hard glare.

‘Don’t stare.’

‘You were staring at me and what the hell is normal about combat on holiday?’

‘I didn’t really mean that,’ I said.

He exhaled.

‘That’s a relief.’

‘But it’s not completely unusual.’ Both his eyes opened again.

'I get the sense you're not joking.'

I played it straight.

'Sometimes, things happen. Circumstances aren't always predictable, like right now.'

'You suddenly have my full attention.'

'John. Johannes. The first time I confronted him, he knew we were coming and I'd left him the Todd surname as a trigger. He was prepared for us. He had a burly guy with a pump-action shotgun on standby.'

'I vaguely remember this.'

I reached over to slap his knee but he was out of reach.

'Loser,' he said.

'The sun is shrinking me.'

He gave a small chuckle then said, 'Go on.'

I took my glass off the table and sipped some water.

'After that, he tried to have the local detectives come to the hotel with the intention of leaning on me, hauling me into jail and getting me thrown out of South Africa.'

'Yes, I figured that was their overall plan.'

'Both attempts were unsuccessful and now the full ultimatum has been delivered...' I let the sentence trail off.

'You're expecting him to run more interference plays?'

'Based on what he's done so far, it would be out of character if he didn't try.'

Oliver considered this for a few moments then he sighed and straightened up in his chair.

'Yeah, I guess you're right.'

I said nothing while I listened to the birds in the bushes around the pool. Eventually, I picked up the conversation again.

'The thing I don't know is how much money he's prepared

to throw at making this problem go away.'

'How much has he got? My experience of people in serious trouble is they'll spend whatever they've got to get out of it.'

'According to my enquiries, between the two of them, he and the winery have around the equivalent of four-point-five million US in cash.'

He exhaled a long, drawn-out breath.

'That buys a lot of interference.'

'Yeah.'

'Is this your not-so-subtle way of telling me that we should get prepared?'

'I'm always prepared,' I said.

'Go on then. Tell me your 'prepared' way out of this.'

'I don't want to get into a shooting war. Guns are too easy to come by in South Africa, easier than in the US. He could drive into town, give half a dozen kids five-hundred bucks each and ask them to give our rental car some extra ventilation when we drive past. That would be the end of the story.'

'That's chump change when you've got four and a half mil in the bank.'

'Yeah. So, like I said, I don't want to get into a shooting war.'

'We'd lose,' he observed. 'Superior numbers will always win.'

'Totally. Instead of a shooting war, I'm going on a charm offensive.'

'He won't let you get close enough to exchange the time of day.'

'No, he won't,' I agreed and took another sip of water.

Chapter 29: Laura

Early the next morning, we headed back towards the winery but, instead of driving all the way up, we pulled off the track and parked inside the tin-roofed barn.

We got out of the car and looked around. The barn probably hadn't been used for a long time. It was open on the long side facing into the field and closed on the other three sides. There was a dusty, dried-up tap in the corner and an old tarpaulin hung from a hook on one end-wall.

'Oh-seven-thirty,' said Oliver.

'Time to break out the MREs.'

'Or the T-Rations,' he said.

'You know you've spent too many hours on standby in the field when you start to fantasise about Meals Ready to Eat and Tray Rations.'

'I love operational food,' he said.

'Really? I did a couple of operations with the Brits.'

'Oh? What do they eat?' he asked. 'Beans on toast?'

'When they're out in the field, they eat a thing called a banjo.'

He chuckled. 'What's a banjo?'

'It's a runny fried egg with three rashers of soft-cooked bacon in a sandwich of really thick bread.'

'Typical Brits, always got the upper hand. That's a meal by itself,' he said.

'It's best eaten at oh-five-thirty, accompanied by a mug of gunfire. Sets you up for whatever the day brings.'

'Gunfire?'

'It's really strong tea with a dash of something illicit.'

'All this at oh-five-thirty? My respect for the Brits just went up a notch,' he said. 'Where? With the Brits?'

'Hot, sandy places.'

'You're secretive.'

'Not really, I just don't like talking about ancient history.'

He nodded slowly as he looked around.

'I don't understand why I didn't run across you in the army.'

'You did, Oliver. You just didn't want to undress me.'

'I doubt that.'

'Nobody wants to undress me in uniform.'

'There are websites dedicated to undressing women in uniform.'

'Speaking from experience, Oliver?'

'I may have carried out some field research during idle moments.'

'The trouble with you, sergeant, you had too many idle moments.'

'I've spent a lot of time hanging around places, waiting for things to happen,' he said.

I smiled.

'And here we are. Hanging around a place, waiting for something to happen,' I said.

'You mind if I sack down?'

'Help yourself. I'll wake you if anything happens.'

He climbed into the car, reclined the seat and settled down.

I leaned back against the driver's door, looked out of the open side of the barn and gazed up at the track that ran across the mountain to the far distant bungalow. I waited.

If you do enough waiting, you get into a sort of rhythm and it becomes easy. Your mind half drifts, you think about things and people and places but a part of you stays anchored on the waiting and the watching. I thought about places I'd waited and times I'd waited.

There was a time in the Russian enclave of Kaliningrad when I'd waited on top of a hill outside Kolovoska. I'd stared down at the heavily camouflaged buildings for five days and six nights. Nothing happened apart from really bad cramp and awkward toilet activity.

I took a deep breath. The air was cooler at this altitude and that took me to another, different wait. I was on a research ship in the Arctic Circle. Too much looking at ice makes you go temporarily blind. I was blind for 24 hours.

Today's wait in South Africa was a dream compared to that.

The almost quiet snoring from inside the car made me smile and then there it was, dust on the track. I reckoned it would take whoever it was around four minutes to get down here to the junction.

I slipped into the driver's seat and started the engine. Oliver woke and looked at me but I just shrugged. He pulled his seat upright and clipped in his seat belt. I took the car onto the track and reversed three hundred metres back the way we'd come.

When I could see the cloud of dust was almost at the barn, I drove forwards. We met the other vehicle, nose-to-nose, at the junction.

I stopped, got out and walked to the truck that had come down the mountain.

It wasn't him. Good.

Nala looked puzzled.

'Hello?'

'It's Laura,' I replied. 'We came-'

‘I know who you are. My father doesn’t like you. Does he know you’re on the way up to see him?’

‘I’m not. I was hoping to catch you.’

‘I don’t think I have anything to say to you. Can you let me pass? I have an appointment in town.’ She wasn’t angry but she wasn’t a pushover. This young woman had bags of confidence and didn’t need to be aggressive to make her point.

‘All I want to do is talk, Nala. It’s important that you understand what’s going on. I don’t want there to be any confusion about the business arrangement your father and I are discussing.’

‘He said you’re a thief and he’s going to stop you.’

‘He’s tried twice.’

Nala looked surprised.

‘He hasn’t told you? About the man with the shotgun? And about sending the police to the hotel to get me thrown out of the country?

‘He’s getting a lawyer to make what you want impossible to get.’

‘If he does, he’s just making an awkward situation into a difficult one with legal problems he’ll have to solve. Can I get in your truck and talk while you drive into town?’

She glanced at her watch; it glittered expensively against her suntanned skin.

‘Are you going to hurt me?’ she asked.

‘No, I have no intention of hurting anyone. Not you, not your father.’

‘What about him?’ She gestured at Oliver in the car in front of her.

‘Oliver couldn’t hurt a fly,’ I lied, because Force Recon Marines just don’t hurt anyone ever.

'He looks like he could.'

'All Oliver wants to do is eat and sleep and, when he's not eating or sleeping, he's thinking about having sex.'

She raised an eyebrow.

'Thinking about it?'

I smiled.

'Maybe doing it, if he's lucky.'

'Does he often get lucky?'

Nala seemed unnecessarily interested in Oliver's sex life.

'If you'll let me ride down with you, we can discuss the arrangement I'm negotiating with your father and, if there's time, we'll talk about Oliver's various appetites.'

I got the feeling she wanted to say yes but she hesitated so I asked a security question.

'Are you armed?'

She hesitated again.

'That's a yes,' I said. 'Take it out from wherever it is and put it on your lap. If you feel unsafe, tell me to get out or shoot me.'

She thought about it for three beats then reached under her seat and dropped a 9mm Vektor semi-automatic pistol into her lap. The way she handled it told me she was comfortable around firearms. Nala was a dangerous young woman.

'Get in,' she said.

I signalled to Oliver that he should follow us then I slid into the passenger seat of her truck.

As she let out the clutch, I started talking. I gave her the whole story, left nothing out. I felt sorry for her because this would change her relationship with her father. He'd put me in a position where I had to start protecting myself and I wanted to do it in a way that didn't leave a trail of bodies all over South Africa.

Chapter 30: Margaret

I was shivering when I woke. I rolled over, peeled back the curtain and ran a finger down the glass. The ice on the inside of the window was thick and lumpy. My breath huffed as I peered into the silent, deep blackness.

'Bible black,' Dylan Thomas had said. He had a way with words.

Thinking of the Welsh poet and his work '*Under Milk Wood*' made my mind drift.

A couple of years ago, I had considered moving the lorry across the border to Wales, somewhere rural but with megaliths close by. I needed to be near my big ancient stones. But nothing had come of that idea. Why move across the border when I could be close to my stones right here?

I hunkered down under the duvet and once more thought about what I'd gain by moving and what I'd lose if I did. I didn't have roots here and yet, the more time I spent thinking about moving away, the bigger the wrench seemed to get. I had lived in this place a long time, longer than some relationships. Longer than some marriages…

I tried to imagine living somewhere else and I couldn't so maybe it *was* time to move on? Maybe it was time to break the connection that had grown around me, the link which had tethered me here while I wasn't looking.

Half an hour of shivering later, I got out of bed. It was so cold that I put two layers of clothes on over my pyjamas, shuffled into the living room, lit the stove and put the kettle on. While I waited for it to boil, I sat in front of the fledgling flames and thought some more about the past.

I had lived, briefly, in the Malvern Hills. Although not in

Wales, they were close to it. The Malverns were nice countryside but they were too near Hereford. That was where we had lived, Harry and I, when he flew for the Regiment. That simple thought opened the door to a time of too many painful memories.

That life was so far away: A different time, a different place, a different person. I had lived this lifestyle for so long that this was 'normal'. The thought of living in one house, in one place, for the rest of my life seemed… odd. I had changed.

I poured the hot water into a mug and wondered when that had happened.

Later, my walk to Little Willy through the crisply starched and white-frosted grass chilled my feet. The naked branches on the trees were half white. Even the patchy red rust on the roof of the old cow byre was covered with a sparkling, white overcoat.

I settled against the ancient stone and closed my eyes. The walk had warmed me and the cold didn't return straight away.

I let my mind float. As sometimes happens, my earlier thoughts and memories led the way. A face flashed in front of me. Long forgotten, it jumped into my consciousness and I wish it hadn't. I didn't hate him; I didn't like him. John the Bastard. His condescending smirk. His 'I know more than you' smile. I don't know how I had found him attractive but I was vulnerable back then.

I tried to let my mind float but he kept returning, looking older each time. I noticed there was another face, half-hidden behind his. A young woman. I couldn't see her clearly but she wouldn't go away.

I opened my eyes to clear my vision and watched my

breath on the cold air in front of me.

I closed my eyes again and, this time, all I could see was my shopping list. Sometimes it works, sometimes it doesn't. I mentally added matches and a note to check the charity shop for warm clothes. Then I tried again. A face took shape. Her face, yes. I was convinced it was the same woman. Asian. Long, dark hair. Deep, dark, troubled - and troubling - eyes. I felt I knew her and yet we'd never met.

The cold began to leak into my bones, telling me it was time to go. I stood, dusted myself off, picked up the blanket and went home. As I walked, I thought about the faces and I wondered about the young woman. What was I being told? I didn't understand, so I tried to focus on mundane things.

A visit to the charity shop was a good idea. I'd make that a priority.

Chapter 31: The Old Man

The meeting took place at the top of a long, mountain road that led to nothing except an unmanned radio tower. The pull-in was empty when he'd arrived an hour ago. He'd walked around the radio tower and out, into the bush, to make sure there were no hikers or campers on the mountainside.

The white Ford Ranger arrived at exactly 1pm. He walked towards it and saw there were two people inside. The passenger got out and looked around. He was a huge man, big like a rugby player. The passenger nodded at him then walked back down the road and around the corner. The driver slid out and walked up to him. They shook hands like old friends.

'Johannes,' he said. 'Good to see you again.'

'Likewise, Damian, likewise.'

They walked to the waist-high, stone wall which bordered the pull-in.

'Even on a day not so clear, the view from up here is still stunning,' said Damian.

'We used to meet here every month,' said Johannes.

'We did. We did some crazy stuff in the old days but they were different times. Everything has changed now.'

'And you are different too? Nearly retired now?' asked Johannes.

'Three months and I'll be gone,' said Damian as he peered over the edge of the mountain.

'I don't want to push you, old friend, but would you be able to do anything about my problem?'

'You mean this American girl and the man she's with?'

'They are trouble. I need them taking care of.'

'What you need, Johannes, is to tread carefully. She is well-connected. She can bring us all a great deal of trouble.'

'You won't help me?'

Damian sighed.

'I can't help you. This is above my head. I can't involve the department and I have little hope of bringing anyone else in from a different police division.'

Johannes turned and perched against the wall.

'I need them dealt with. What do you suggest?'

'How much trouble can they cause for you?'

'I could lose everything, Damian. My house, my farm, the winery.'

Damian said nothing while he thought it through.

‘If things went wrong and there was an investigation into your status, it would bring someone to my door. They’d discover how you got your citizenship. It would lead them to me,’ he said.

‘I told you they were trouble.’

‘Can you pay them off? Everyone has their price.’

‘They don’t want money.’

‘Really?’ said Damian. ‘That is unusual. What do they want?’

‘Reparation for something I did in England a long time ago.’

‘Can you not do what they want?’

‘I could, Damian, but that would cause problems at home. Nala would want to know why I was giving part of the business away and why I was bringing in an outsider as a co-owner. She would want to know why I was sending money each month to someone in England. I would have no good answer to the questions she would ask.’

Damian was silent while he thought things over.

Eventually, he spoke again.

‘You see, the thing is, Johannes, I can’t help. The police service is not what it was. There is scrutiny now, oversight and authorisation. I answer to people who are not as… flexible as we were a few decades ago. Even getting a team to go and interview these two, that almost got me suspended. When the call came through from the Director of the National Intelligence Agency asking why I had sent detectives to interview a member of the US intelligence community-’

‘What?’

‘She works for the Office of the President of the United

States. According to our NIA she is on his staff of intelligence advisors.'

'Shit.'

'I can't help you on this one, Johannes. I could get exposed. I could lose my job, my pension. I could lose everything.'

Johannes put his head in his hands.

'I'm in trouble then.'

'If you can't make peace with her then yes, you're in deep trouble.'

'Can you help me find someone who could take care of them?'

'I would counsel against trying to find anyone who could help. It could end very badly for both of us.'

'Is that your final advice?'

'No, Johannes. My final advice would be to settle with them. If anything happened to two American intelligence agents in Cape Town, it would throw up a lot of dust. There would be Government enquiries. My part in trying to arrest them would come out and I would be under suspicion of being involved in corruption. I would be investigated. I'm not spotless, my friend. They would find something from my past, probably several somethings. Such an investigation would not end well for me.'

Neither spoke for what seemed a long time. Johannes broke the silence.

'I could go to Pretoria. Hire someone to come and take care of them? Someone independent?'

'You could but you're not understanding something, Johannes. There would still be an investigation. It would lead to my attempt to arrest them after you called me. We both thought these were ordinary Americans but they're not. I think your only way out of this is to settle with them. Give them what they want.'

He checked his watch. It was time to go. He sent a text and his passenger walked back into sight.

Damian put his arm around Johannes' shoulder.

'I'm sorry, old friend, but my advice is my last word on this. Give them what they ask for. It won't hurt you. And it's the best way to make this problem go away.'

'I can't,' said Johannes. 'I just can't. It would cause too many problems at home.'

Damian nodded over his shoulder and the passenger walked up behind them. He grabbed Johannes' chin and the back of his head, twisting upward and sideways in a practiced move. The soft, crunching click of breaking bone was audible.

Johannes dropped like a stone.

The passenger hauled Johannes' corpse onto his shoulders, carried him to the edge of the pull-in and threw his body into the deep gorge below.

'I gave him the way out of the problem,' said Damian, as they walked back to the Ford Ranger. 'He should have taken it.'

Chapter 32: Laura

The telephone woke me. My watch said it was 06:23. I picked up the handset.

'Miss Guerra, this is reception. You have a visitor who needs to see you urgently.'

'Now?'

'She says it is most urgent.'

'Who is it?'

'Her name is Nala.'

'And she's here? Now?'

'Waiting at reception.'

'OK. I'll come right down.'

I hung up, slipped out of bed, pulled on my bathrobe and a pair of slippers and brushed the worst tangles out of my hair. Oliver was still asleep, sprawled across most of the bed. I picked up the key card, left the room and walked towards the main entrance.

She was standing in front of the reception desk.

'Morning,' I said.

'My dad's gone.'

I blinked and thought about that.

'Gone as in he's run away?'

'No. He's disappeared.'

'Let's talk somewhere more comfortable.' I turned to the receptionist. 'Can we have a coffee and a pot of tea in the lounge, please?'

The receptionist picked up a phone to pass the order to the kitchen.

'Follow me,' I said to Nala, and I led the way.

We sat at a table by some open French doors. The scents from the garden filtered into the room on the gentle morning breeze.

'Talk to me,' I said.

'I got home after lunch,' said Nala. 'He wasn't there, his truck was gone. I waited for him. I wanted to ask him about everything you'd told me. I was angry and I wanted to hear things from him, not from you.'

'Understandable.'

'He didn't come home. I waited up until midnight and he's never that late to bed when he's staying at home. I rang the police and they said they'd treat the report as a missing person. I don't need a missing person report to know something's wrong.'

'Does he have any friends? Anyone he might have gone to stay with?'

'No, he's a solitary man. After my mother died, he withdrew to the house and the winery. He goes away once a year to the trade conference. He doesn't have friends.'

'What about a club he might have stayed at? A golf club or-'

'No clubs. No friends. He doesn't have any family except for me.'

'What about people he might have worked with in the past? Former colleagues?'

'No. We've lived at the winery since before I was born. We used to have a farm manager but he died a few years ago.'

We paused the conversation while a waiter brought our drinks and set them out on the table.

I thought about how Johannes lived a solitary life, then I tried to square that with how he had become a South African citizen through the acquisition of false papers. Somewhere in the past, he had known someone. Someone had known him.

'There must be somebody,' I said. 'A person he might have been close to once?'

'Nobody,' she said. 'The only people we get Christmas cards from are each other. There isn't anyone he could have spent the night with.'

I sipped my tea and asked the obvious question.

'Why have you come to me, Nala?'

'Because it seems you know more about my father than I do. I'm hoping you'd know where he might have gone.'

It took a lot of guts to say that but it took more guts to come and find me.

'Is there a favourite place?' I asked. 'Somewhere he goes when he wants to think things through?'

'I can't think of any but we used to go to the beach for picnics when I was young.'

'There are a lot of beaches in Cape Town,' I mused.

'We haven't been on a picnic for fifteen years.'

'Doesn't seem likely then,' I said. 'Drink your coffee. Would you like breakfast?'

'I'm not hungry.'

'When did you last eat?'

'I had lunch yesterday.'

I signalled the waiter and asked for the breakfast menu.

'You need to eat. You can't think properly if you're hungry.'

She waved away the menu.

'Two poached eggs, toast. Another coffee,' she said.

'I'll have the Full English,' I said. 'And another pot of tea.'

The waiter walked away to organise our food.

'Where's your friend?' she asked.

'He's still asleep, probably dreaming about food.'

'Does he do much sleeping?'

'He's trained to sleep. It's one of the things he does well.'

I wanted to get the conversation back on track.

'Your father's car, does it have a tracker fitted?'

'No, nothing like that.'

'What about him, does he have a mobile phone?'

'Yes, it's aways with him but it's very old.'

'How old?'

'About ten years, maybe more,' said Nala.

I sighed.

'It doesn't seem like we are going to have much luck tracking him.'

'No, not much,' she said.

'Did you check for his papers? ID card? Passport?'

'No, I didn't think to.'

'OK then. When we've eaten, I'll get dressed and we can go to your house to look for things which might be missing.'

For the first time since I'd come downstairs, she gave the briefest smile.

Chapter 33: Laura

Nala drove us back to the winery in silence, her mind locked in a world of her own creation. Oliver followed in the rental. At the bungalow, Nala got out and unlocked a side door.

'Come in. Tell your friend he's welcome too.'

I gestured for Oliver to follow us.

We walked into a large, well-equipped kitchen. I was impressed at someone's culinary ambitions.

'I'll go and look for his passport,' she said as she disappeared through double doors.

'I'll come with you,' I said, following. I subtly signalled for Oliver to look around.

Nala took a seat behind a desk in a neat, little office,

adjoining the comfortable lounge. She was opening drawers, shuffling things around and looking frustrated.

'It's usually here,' she said. I could feel her impatience building.

'How about I go through the desk while you go and check his bedroom for any missing clothes?'

She looked up at me for a few moments.

'Okay but shout if you find it.'

'I will. You shout if you see something unusual.'

I was careful, methodical, and soon found the passport in a side drawer underneath some bank statements. I flicked through the green booklet and saw it was due to expire in four years. I wondered why a man who had never travelled outside South Africa (if you believed him) would have a passport in the first place and why would he keep it up to date? It looked unused and there were no stamps inside.

I leafed through the bank statements. They were for his personal account. Johannes kept a moderate credit balance. Some transactions had pencil lines through them while others had a little tick against the amount. The transactions all seemed to be regular, routine payments.

I tidied the statements, put them back in the drawer and walked back into the dining room.

'Found the passport!' I called out.

Nala jogged in. I handed it to her.

'He always takes it with him when he goes travelling,' she said.

'Why?'

'Why, what?'

'Why does he have a passport? Why does he take it with him?'

'Oh, I see. Dad doesn't like the Identity Cards. He's always losing his. He's lost at least six, that I'm aware of. He uses his passport as proof of identity when he buys guns or ammunition.'

That was interesting.

'Does he carry a gun?' I asked.

'Yes, a Vektor SP-One, the same as mine. He often leaves it in the truck but he has a belt holster and wears the gun in the small of his back.'

'Is his gun here?'

'Looking for it wouldn't tell us much. He's hardly ever brought it into the house. It is either in the truck or on his belt.'

I filed that information away. Oliver walked in from the kitchen.

'Find anything?' I asked.

'There's some pineapple cake in the fridge.'

Sometimes, being around Oliver was like being with a small child.

'Anything else?'

'Milk, cream, two melons, a bowl of strawberries. Some ham, yoghurt and sausages.'

See what I mean? A small child.

'I didn't mean in the fridge…'

'Oh, right. Well, no, the kitchen looks like a kitchen. Everything neat, nothing out of place, no sign of a struggle.'

'Struggle?' asked Nala.

'Well, yeah,' explained Oliver. 'If he's gone, you should consider the possibility that he didn't leave of his own accord.'

Nala suddenly looked like she might burst into tears so I tried to brush over what Oliver had said.

'From what I've seen of the house so far, that's not likely. It looks like he just walked out, got in his truck and drove off.'

Nala gulped for air a few times while she got herself back under control.

'Keys,' she said. 'The spare keys for the truck are still here; his keys are gone.'

'See what I mean?' I said. 'He's just gone out somewhere.'

'But it's not like him. He's never spent the night away from home before, except for wine trade meetings, and there aren't any more of those this year.'

'We could try calling the hospitals?' I offered. 'Maybe he was taken unwell while he was out from the house.'

'That's not a bad idea,' Oliver jumped in. 'I'll make a list of the Cape Town hospitals and we can start calling them.'

'How are you going to do that?' asked Nala.

'The internet,' he replied as he got his phone out.

'There's almost no signal up here. Use the laptop in the office. It's slow but it will be quicker than your phone.'

'Right, thanks,' he said. Then, he looked confused.

'Through there.' She pointed at the doorway into the office.

''Kay, thanks.'

'So, his gun is probably in the truck; the truck is gone but his passport is here. Did you find anything in the bedroom that might help?'

'The clothes he was wearing yesterday are gone. Everything else looks normal. His hiking boots aren't here but I think he was wearing those when he went out.'

'Did you look in the bathroom?'

'I checked his en-suite. His toothbrush and razor are there.'

'Hmm. This is looking more and more like he's stepped out and something's happened to him. We'll wait until Oliver has the list of hospitals and then we'll get calling.'

She gave me a wan smile.

Chapter 34: Laura

Nala and I walked into the kitchen where she made coffee for herself and tea for me. We were leaning against the worktop, not really saying much, when Oliver walked in. He had compiled a list of medical establishments in Cape Town. The large hospitals with ERs were at the top of the list, community medical centres at the bottom.

'I'll start calling,' I said. 'Can I use the house phone?'

'Sure. There's a handset on the table in the lounge.'

I gave Oliver a warning stare as I walked past him and he winked back at me. It took over an hour to call all of the numbers on the list. I gave everyone the same information: a description of Johannes, his full name and date of birth and the approximate time he was last seen. There were no matches to my query.

I put the handset down, stared into space. I was wondering about calling the mortuary directly when Oliver and Nala walked in. He carried two plates, a slice of cake on each.

'You should try this,' he said. 'It's better than the best thing you've ever eaten.'

He put one of the plates in front of me then attacked his slice of cake with enthusiasm. I would have preferred a glass of water but I nibbled at the cake.

'Wow,' I enthused. 'This is really good. Are you the baker?'

She looked embarrassed; a blush began to rise through her

cheeks.

'I cook everything. Dad is terrible in the kitchen. He can burn baked beans and incinerate toast.'

'So, the kitchen is your domain?'

'We had it fitted out as a business expense. I wanted a kitchen I could cook in, as well as be creative and experimental.'

I raised an eyebrow at the word 'experimental' but she didn't want to talk about cooking. I filled her in on the calls.

'I'm afraid there's no report of him being admitted anywhere,' I summed up.

She walked to the desk and picked up the handset.

'I need to call the police again,' she said and began dialling the number.

Oliver caught my eye. We walked into the kitchen with our plates while Nala waited to speak to someone. I drew a glass of water from the tap while Oliver quietly updated me.

'The search history on the laptop gave me a name,' he said. 'He looked for the office number of a guy called Damian Hout. You'll like this: the exact search was "Damian Hout senior detective Cape Town police".'

'Well, that is very interesting,' I said. 'Are you going to tell me he ran that search a few hours before our visitors arrived at the hotel?'

'You're so sharp, it's a wonder you don't cut yourself.'

'Did you learn anything else?' I asked.

'He Googled you.'

'I'm not surprised. Not you?'

'He doesn't know my name and searching the Internet for "handsome sexual dynamo" wouldn't be productive.'

I spluttered into my glass of water.

'Anything else?'

'He has a deep fondness for semi-automatic weapons. A careful search of the house might throw up a few surprises, but there was nothing else interesting on the laptop.'

'Just a love of semi-automatic weapons and looking up the contact number of a senior detective,' I said.

'And a lot of stuff about wine exports.'

We stopped talking as we heard Nala end the call. She walked into the kitchen, looking like she might be about to cry.

'They have him recorded as a missing person but they won't mount a search or anything, even though this disappearance is out of character.'

I felt like I should comfort her but that wouldn't have been appropriate. Oliver surprised me.

'Nala, we are due to leave South Africa at the end of next week but we'll spend some time looking for him before we go,' he said.

She gave him a look I couldn't quite label.

'That would be nice, thank you. But what could you do?'

'I'm sure he's going to turn up. In the meantime, Oliver and I could make some enquiries for you. Maybe we'll think of something you haven't considered?'

She gave him a *look* that was older than apple-picking, and a small piece of the puzzle dropped into place. She was interested in him.

'That would be very nice of you.' She switched her gaze to me. 'Of you both. I would be grateful of anything you could do.'

I thought about it for a moment.

'I guess you don't want to leave the house right now. Is there anything you need? Can we arrange for anything to be brought up here?'

'The freezers are well-stocked but I could do with some fresh food? Vegetables, some milk and eggs. I was going to go down the mountain and buy those today but…' She let the sentence hang.

'No problem,' I said. 'Leave that to us. We'll bring some up tomorrow.'

I slipped my jacket on and asked if I could use the toilet. She showed me where the family bathroom was and went back to the kitchen.

When I rejoined them, I made sure we all had each other's numbers. She saw us to the door and watched us drive away before going back inside. Oliver drove.

'She's a sweet kid,' he said, looking in the rear-view mirror.

'She's desperate for some attention and she's emotionally on edge.'

'What do you think has happened to him?'

'Two plus two equals four. I think Senior Detective Damian Hout has questions to answer.'

'How are you going to do that?'

'I'll have a little chat with him,' I said as I placed the Beretta M9 and two 17-round magazines from my coat pocket on my lap.

He glanced down at them then cocked an eye at me.

'You were right about his fondness for semi-automatic weapons,' I said. 'These were on the top shelf of his wardrobe.'

'Well, that's a good conversation opener,' he said.

I nodded as the car bumped its way back down the track.

Chapter 35: Laura

The internet told us that Senior Detective Damian Hout was based in a regional office, north-west of the centre of Cape Town. The address led us to a single-storey industrial unit. The squat building sat behind a 3-metre-high steel fence. I drove around the unit twice. Oliver was spotter. After the second lap, I pulled into a nearby side street, switched the engine off and sipped some bottled water while he briefed me.

'No windows, one fortified main doorway, a discrete sign that says "reception". Three fire exits. The anti-climb fence runs around the building. There are no overhanging trees. They have cameras every twenty metres around the perimeter and - here's the clever bit - there are cameras on the corner of every building on the roads opposite.'

I thought about it for a moment, then took another sip of water before I spoke.

'Kind of makes you wonder what sort of detecting this detective division does.'

'After looking at that office, I'm guessing they don't work on domestic disputes,' he said.

'I reckon Senior Detective Damian Hout and his team don't have many friends in the world of organised crime.'

'Yeah. Doesn't it seem odd that a successful wine producer would be keen to speak to a senior detective?'

'Maybe Johannes found a criminal conspiracy in the wine trade,' I thought aloud.

'Or maybe they're buddies from the bad old days?'

'They could be buddies from the bad old days,' I agreed. 'We need to know what he looks like. I'm thinking of walking in there and saying hello.'

Oliver's intake of breath made me smile.

'On the one hand, that's a ballsy move and I sort of agree with you. On the other hand, you're talking about putting your head in the lion's den,' he said.

'Mouth. Head in the lion's mouth.'

'I knew that.'

I mulled it over.

'Detective Hout sent that team to the hotel, right?'

'Seems likely it was him,' Oliver agreed.

'And he's not expecting us to turn up at his station.'

'That would be very unexpected.'

'He might get a little flustered if we did rock up and ask him how it's hanging?'

'Hmmm… I don't want to disagree…'

'But?'

'Yeah, but… but he's a senior detective in a front-line division. I don't think he'll fall to his knees and give you an instant confession.'

'I said we might get him flustered. I'm not expecting him to crack like an egg,' I countered.

'We understand each other.'

'We do but I'm going to hit him where he's not expecting to be hit.'

'Where's that?'

'I'm going to hit his self-confidence.'

Chapter 36: Laura

We parked in a side street and walked into the compound. The reception doors remained shut as we approached so I gestured to the intercom on the wall. Oliver pushed the button and a tinny voice responded.

'Can I help you?'

I checked out the CCTV cameras above our heads.

'Mel Brooks to see Detective Damian Hout.'

I raised an eyebrow at the false name.

'What's it concerning?'

'I need to speak to Detective Hout about that… I have important information for him.'

There was a pause while consultation happened behind the scenes.

'Come to reception please,' said the tinny voice.

The doors slid open.

'Bulletproof glass and heavy-duty steel,' I muttered. Oliver would have noted the strength of the doors as well.

We walked through a short corridor. An identical set of sliding doors waited at the far end. As soon as the outer doors had closed, the inner doors opened, admitting us into reception. The large room was sparsely furnished. Ahead of us was a wall with a 2-metre square glass panel set in it. Two staff in civilian clothing sat behind the glass panel. They both wore handguns in hip holsters.

We walked up to the glass panel.

'Help you?' asked one of them through an intercom.

'Mel Brooks for Detective Hout,' said Oliver.

'He's on his way. He said to wait in interview room two.' She pointed at a door with a large '2' on it.

We walked into the room. A metre-and-a-half deep table filled the left-to-right floorspace, three chairs on our side, two chairs on the far side as well as another door set in the back wall. Three cameras covered all the angles.

Out of habit, I tried the door handle behind us. It wouldn't open.

'Automatic lock,' I said.

'They don't like people walking in, they don't like people walking out.'

'You ever seen security this tight in a civilian police station before?' I asked.

He chuckled and shook his head as the door in front of us opened. A tall, late middle-aged man walked in. He wore an expensive, dark-coloured suit over a white shirt and red tie, black shoes on his feet. He did not look like a typical detective.

'How may I help you, Mister Brooks?' he asked.

'Actually, I'm the one who's here to see you, Detective Hout,' I said. 'My name is Laura Guerra; I believe you may have heard the name?'

For a fraction of a second, he froze. His body language struggled to recover; his face lagged behind.

'I can't say I have, Miss Guerra,' he lied.

'You didn't send a team of detectives to my hotel? The investigation notes I've read mentioned you by name, Detective Hout.'

'What investigation notes would those be, Miss Guerra?'

'The investigation that the National Intelligence Agency is running.' I lied. Sue me.

His face briefly showed shock so I hit him with another blow.

'Where's Johannes Marula?'

Colour seemed to drain from his face so I hit him again.

'We know you have spoken with him twice in the last couple of weeks. We know you arranged to meet him and he hasn't been seen since. Where is Johannes Marula?'

He grasped for words. He wasn't having a good day.

'Who… Who sent you?'

'Where is John Procera, the man you provided with the identity of Johannes Marula?'

He began to get a grip on himself.

'I have no idea who or what you are talking about, Miss Guerra. I don't think we have anything further to discuss.'

He reached under the desk and the door behind us buzzed before popping open.

'Please leave this division. If you return, I will have you arrested for wasting police time.'

'I'll be back, Detective Hout, but I'll be back with arresting officers when the investigation into an attempt to falsely detain us concludes. Tomorrow?' I looked at Oliver for confirmation.

'Paper's due back tomorrow,' he joined in with the bluffing game.

'We'll see you the day after tomorrow then,' I said.

I turned and walked out of the interview room and into reception. Oliver followed me out of the building.

We got into the car and exhaled all the pressure out of our bodies.

'That was intense,' he said.

'I imagine it was more intense for him.'

'He's as guilty as hell,' said Oliver.

'Yep,' I agreed. 'We put him off balance and he's got himself backed into a corner. He thinks he's being investigated. We have accused him of being complicit in someone's disappearance and he thinks his past of supplying false identities is catching up with him. I'm as sure as hell he didn't do it just the once.'

'I'd go along with that. If you had a nice way of making extra cash, you'd keep turning the handle on the money-making machine,' he said.

'I think what we have to do is figure out what his next move is going to be. We need to get in the way before he makes it,' I said.

'Seeing as how his world is imploding,' said Oliver 'My best guess would be "get the hell out of the country".'

'I agree. Speaking of getting out of the country, how's your holiday going?'

'The food is good; the sex is first class, but other things are just getting exciting.'

Chapter 37: Laura

We agreed we needed to split up, to double our presence on the ground, so I drove onto the main street and parked where I had a view of the building's main entrance. Oliver got out and hailed a taxi. I staked out reception just in case Damian Hout left early. I figured that the high security meant there probably wasn't an alternate way for staff to get in and out. I've worked in a few similar places and only one had a super-secret back entrance.

I bet you smirked at 'back entrance', didn't you?

Less than an hour later, Oliver tapped on the window. I flipped the ignition on and wound the window down.

'Hey, gorgeous. Are you looking for a good time?'

'Well, that depends. Do you have a gallon of baby oil and a packet of flavoured condoms?'

'Laura, I'm seeing you in a whole new light.'

'No, you're not,' I said. 'You're just figuring out where you can get a gallon of baby oil from.'

'You know me too well.'

'What did you get and where did you park it?' I asked.

'I took the best the hire company had; it's a grey, year-old Chrysler SUV. I'm parked on the opposite road. It gives me the same view of the entrance.'

'Excellent choice of wheels, Oliver.'

'No show yet?'

'Three out, two in, none of them our man,' I answered.

'Burning the telephone up?'

'That sounds a reasonable guess.'

'In that case, I'll get back to the car. I'll call you so we can keep an open channel,' he said.

'Drive carefully, dear.'

'I'm still thinking about a gallon of baby oil, you know.'

I watched him walk away. I was going to miss Oliver. Beneath his tough but laid-back exterior lurked a really sweet guy just waiting for the right person to come along. He'd already said he was heading back to Whiteland for another six-month contract, while I had to get to the UK once I'd sorted things out in South Africa.

Thoughts of the UK took me to Margaret. I wondered how she was doing. I was due to revisit her in a couple of months but, before that, I had to visit someone in Hereford. More pressingly, though, I needed the situation in South Africa sorted out.

The phone rang.

'How many times have I told you never to call me here?'

'I was only going to ask if the gallon of baby oil is compulsory,' he said.

'Just bring yourself and a bucketful of enthusiasm. I'm feeling frisky.'

'Lady, I'm going to do my very best to satisfy your friskiness.'

'I'm counting on it. I have an itch and it needs some serious scratching.'

'I could come over and give you a little relief?' he offered.

'Don't you dare. I'm on edge as it is.'

We both said 'contact' at the same moment as Damian Hout walked out of the industrial unit. He got in a dirty, white, Ford Ranger truck. It didn't move straight away so I reckoned he was on the phone or maybe waiting for someone.

A few minutes later, I had my answer as a mountain of a man walked out of reception and got in the passenger side of the Ranger. It pulled out of the car park, turned right and drove northwards. I let Oliver take point and pulled in three cars behind him.

After a mile of lefts and rights, the Ranger joined a bigger road, still heading north.

'He's on the freeway,' said Oliver. 'There's not a lot of traffic to mask me. You want to take point for a while?'

'No worries,' I said and moved up until I was two cars behind the Ranger.

Oliver accelerated and, about half a mile ahead, he pulled

into the same lane as our little convoy. That was smart thinking: hardly anyone thinks they're being followed by a car in front.

After about 20 kilometres, the Ranger took an exit ramp without signalling. I didn't think we'd been blown. I hoped the lack of signalling was down to laziness, not a deliberate attempt to mislead us. Unfortunately, Oliver was too far ahead and committed to continue north.

I followed the truck onto a minor road and stayed with it for a few hundred metres but I had no traffic to cover me. To avoid being made, I pulled into a truck stop and watched the Ranger disappear into the distance.

'Lost them,' I said. 'They took a side road on the eastern side of the freeway but still heading north.'

'I'm about six kilometres north of the exit ramp you took. There's an exit ahead. I'll let you know how the land looks in a minute.'

When the Ranger was out of sight, I pulled onto the road and followed the direction it had taken. After two and a half kilometres, the road took a 90-degree right, straightened for 250-metres, then took a 90-degree left before continuing north. After the second hairpin, the road divided. The main part continued north but a small, dusty track disappeared eastwards across the dry fields.

I pulled over, popped the hood and waited.

'OK,' said Oliver. 'I've left the freeway. I'm driving south on what I think is the road you said the Ranger took.'

'We want to know where they went. If Damian is going to skip the country, it'll happen in the next twenty-four hours.'

There was a long pause while Oliver thought about things.

'There is an alternative,' he said.

‘What’s that?’

‘South Africa is a pretty big country. Maybe he’s not going to skip out. Maybe he’s got a place to lay low for a couple of years or so. Maybe all he has to do is get off the radar.’

I didn’t need to think about that for long.

‘You could be right. We don’t know what resources he can call on and we don’t know how much wealth he’s got tucked away.’

‘I’m not just a pretty face?’

I laughed.

‘You are many things, Oliver. I’m not sure “pretty face” is one of them but I’ll make a point of looking closely at it next time we’re in a darkened room.’

‘Are you trying to hurt my feelings?’

‘No. Now, concentrate on the job. I’ll sort out your feelings later.’

‘I’ve found them.’

Chapter 38: Laura

It was an airstrip. The faded sign at the head of the dirt-track said *Die Onafhanklike Vliegklub* which I translated as Independent Flying Club.

We left my car at the pull-in. I got into Oliver’s SUV and we headed up the road, onto the track. Three kilometres later, we arrived at an airstrip that had been carved into the side of an impressive hill. In front of the runway were two aged mobile homes. One looked like someone lived in it while the other had the same Flying Club signwriting on it.

On the far side of the runway were four open-ended hangars and a large one that had huge doors on each end. I counted nine light aircraft and two helicopters parked on this side of the runway. The light aircraft were mostly Piper Cherokee types: good for flying instruction, good for solo flights. The helicopters were next to the office; a Robinson R44 and a Bell B206 Jet Ranger.

'I don't know much about aviation hardware but that looks expensive,' said Oliver as he pointed at the Bell.

'An early nineteen-eighties model would cost about five times what Whiteland are paying you a year.'

'And the fixed-wings?'

'A well-used Piper would cost you six month's salary,' I said.

'I'm now wondering how much a senior detective in Cape Town makes.'

'Hold your horses. We don't even know this is where he came.'

Oliver tutted loudly and said, 'I spy with my little eye, something beginning with "Ford Ranger".'

I looked around. Peeping out from behind the lived-in-looking mobile home was the same truck we'd followed out of Cape Town.

'Nobody,' I said. 'Absolutely nobody likes a smart-ass.'

'You do.'

'Yes. I do but who said I'm not nobody?'

He slowed down to look at me with unblinking eyes.

'It's too late in the afternoon and I'm too hungry for deep, meaningful conversations on the nature of existence.'

'We should definitely find somewhere nice to eat. We deserve a reward,' I said.

He grunted agreement and swung the SUV into a slot in

front of the office-looking building. Before we got out, I checked the Beretta M9 and magazines.

'You expecting trouble?'

'I'm expecting resistance to a bunch of questions.'

'He's a career cop. An M-Nine isn't going to frighten him.'

'It will in my hands. Anyway, I need you to watch my back. Remember the mountain who got in the Ranger with him? He's going to be here somewhere.'

He grinned.

'I shall definitely be watching your ass.'

'Back, Oliver. You need to be watching my back.'

I stepped out, tucked the M9 into the back of my trousers and headed for the office door. Inside, unsurprisingly, was a general aviation office. I've seen hundreds of them. General aviation offices are all different and yet all the same. There were a few uncomfortable-looking folding chairs and two tattered armchairs. Stuck along the walls were faded aviation maps with airways marked out. There was a NOTAM pinboard featuring not 'notices to airmen' but a two-year-old calendar starring ladies of improbable bust size. Below, against the long wall, was a desk which seemed to be held together by thousands of linked-up, coffee-cup rings. Set in the short wall was a window, bordered by tatty lace curtains. The window hadn't been cleaned this year; the lace curtains hadn't been washed in a decade.

Below the window was another, shorter desk cluttered with papers, a desk-lamp, a landline telephone, a mobile telephone and a desktop computer that Noah might have installed on his Ark.

The woman behind the desk wore an Australian Bushman's hat, khaki shirt and denim jeans so ancient they looked almost white. Perhaps they were white, once upon a time.

'Can I help you folks?' She had a clipped accent but the South African twang overlaid something else.

'We're looking for a friend,' I said. 'Damian. Damian Hout. He said we should meet him here.'

'He arrived not long ago. He's probably at Alpha Delta. You'll find her behind the largest hangar. You can drive over, if you don't want the walk. There are no movements scheduled for the next hour.'

I thought it would be polite to have a conversation with her.

'Thanks, it'll be good to see him again. How many aircraft are based here?'

'Fourteen light aircraft, three and a half rotaries.'

'Half?'

She laughed.

'There's a project helicopter in the large hangar. If the owner thinks they'll ever get it in the air, I'm a Dutchman.'

Her half-buried accent clicked into place.

'You're not Dutch, though,' I said. 'Strine?'

She smiled widely.

'That's a good shout. Sydney, born and bred.'

'It's a long way from Sydney to a flying club in South Africa,' I said.

'Not if you make some back-to-back bad choices.' She smiled as she said it. I liked her. I felt she had stories to tell.

She gave me an appraising look.

'You fly?'

'I've held the controls on a few types,' I answered, not quite dishonestly. Being a veteran helicopter and fixed-wing pilot for combat special forces means I've held the controls on a few types, right?

'Well, if you ever want to give it a go for real, give me a shout. I'm the owner and chief instructor of this college of aviation.'

'I'd like that. If we get the time, I'll give you a call?'

'I'll keep the kettle warm,' she said.

Behind me, Oliver opened the door. I followed him outside.

Chapter 39: Laura

'Walk or drive?'

'Drive,' I said. 'I want the cover.'

Oliver drove us across the runway and turned the car towards the rear of the large hangar. He pulled to a stop at the corner of the building.

'Cover's no good if it's too exposed to be cover,' he said, giving me a wink.

I slid out, checked the M9 was still in place beneath my jacket and walked into the hangar, aware that I was entering a danger zone.

There were three and a half aircraft inside. A Piper Commanche, a stunning Diamond DA62 and an elderly Beechcraft King Air 200. There didn't seem to be any people around. The "half" was a Bell 429 Global Ranger helicopter or various parts of her. I could see what the woman in the office had meant. I reckoned a team of mechanics working full time with an unlimited budget might be able to get the

Global Ranger ready for flight in... maybe three years? I doubted a hobbyist would ever finish the job.

There was no noise in the hangar, no signs or sounds of someone working on anything. I walked out and around the back to the far side of the hangar.

I saw two things, three if you count a flash in my peripheral vision.

The first thing I noticed was that Alpha Delta was a South African-registered Piaggio P166, a twin-engine cargo/commuter aircraft. The backwards-facing turbo-prop engine on each side and high set wings are unusual design features which make the P166 stunningly different from almost every other type of aircraft in the world.

The second thing I noticed was that the P166's fuselage door was open. I could see crates inside and Damian Hout was crouching down behind one.

My body reacted instinctively to the brief flash in my peripheral vision. I ducked into a forward roll and something swept down through the space I had been standing in. As I hit the ground, I flipped the forward roll into a side roll away from where that something had come from, before springing to my feet in a ready stance.

'You have a belt!' said the mountain.

'I have a few belts. I also have braces,' I said, ever the master of witty repartee.

He rushed towards me and, faced with a large, muscle-bound man rushing at me, I did the honourable thing. I whipped out the M9 and shot him in the thigh. He howled and went down, clutching his injury. I frisked his writhing body and removed a Vektor Z88 9mm semi-automatic pistol from his belt holster. I threw it back towards the hangar.

I walked to the side of the P166 to keep out of range of the open fuselage door.

'Mister Hout,' I called out. 'We need a chat.'

'Are you going to shoot me too?'

'No, I just want to talk. Besides, you've probably got something lethal on you. How about you toss that out here before we have our discussion?'

There was a long pause, then a gun was thrown out and pitched onto the concrete. A Chinese QSZ-92 9mm semi-automatic. I hadn't tried one of those yet but I'd heard a lot about them.

'Now the other one,' I called out.

'I don't have another,' he said.

'Yes, you do. You have a Vektor Z-Eighty-Eight, just like your colleague out here. That's standard issue in the South African Police, isn't it?'

I flicked a glance back to the mountain. He was still clutching his knee, not giving me the friendliest of looks. Oliver walked out of the hangar and picked up his weapon. I signalled that the open doorway was a threat so he stepped sideways and approached the Piaggio's tail.

'Come on, Detective, toss it out here,' I tried again.

After a long pause, a Vektor Z88 flew out of the doorway. I ducked down and saw Oliver's feet on the other side of the Piaggio, opposite the door.

'I'm coming in now,' I called. 'Let's not do anything silly.'

He didn't answer. Then, breaking the silence, three sharp taps, metal on glass. I whirled into the open doorway as Damian turned to the window behind him, raising a shotgun to his shoulder. I shot him in the right shoulder, lowered my aim and put a hole in the back of his left thigh; two quick shots.

'He's down,' I called to Oliver.

I climbed into the aircraft and squatted down onto my heels.

'You've put a lot of effort into getting away, Damian. What's going on?'

He slowly half-rolled towards me. He groaned with the effort it took to roll over. There was no exit wound in his shoulder but the front of his thigh looked a mess. I took the shotgun he'd dropped and tossed it further inside the aircraft.

Oliver appeared and leaned against the open doorway.

'Yeah,' he said. 'We just wanted to talk to you. If you've been a naughty boy, you'll just get a slap on the wrist.'

'Unless you've been a really, really naughty boy,' I said. 'Tell us about Johannes.'

He groaned a little more as he settled onto his back. He didn't speak while he was getting comfortable.

Eventually, Damian sighed heavily and said, 'Johannes was a good friend.'

That was all the confirmation I needed.

Nala's father was dead.

Chapter 40: Laura

'Where is he?' I asked.

There was a long pause before he answered. 'The radio transmitter, north-west of Elephant's Eye Cave. We used to meet there. Sometimes just to talk, sometimes to discuss business.'

'What "business", Damian?'

Another long pause.

'We moved things. I had connections. He could store things, move things. We used his wine shipping as a legitimate cover. It was easy. We flew cargo out of the country. Sometimes, we'd do it for other people. Sometimes, we'd do it for us. We were never greedy, though. Just did enough.'

'What things did you move?' I had already guessed the answer.

'Gold,' he said. 'Ingots. Krugerrands. Diamonds. Some silver.'

'People, Damian?'

He didn't answer.

'Oliver, I think we need an ambulance for these two.'

'Do we, though?'

I looked at him.

'I think we have a choice of how we deal with them,' he explained.

'Let's think about it; see what's inside the crates.'

'I'll get something to open them.'

He walked back to the hangar and returned with a crowbar.

The six crates were spread out evenly across the inside of the Piaggio. No stranger to moving things by air, Damian had placed his cargo carefully.

The first crate held a dozen 2kg bags of white powder.

'I didn't expect that,' he said.

'Currency,' I replied. 'It's all currency to someone, somewhere. What is that? About twenty-four kilos total?'

He picked up one of the bags and weighed it in his hand.

'About that.'

‘Street value of about two-point-five million US. Let’s try crate number two.’

The second crate contained 30 boxes of Krugerrands, 5 in each box.

‘The Krugers are about eighteen-hundred each,’ I said. ‘That crate is worth a quarter of a million.’

‘American?’ asked Oliver.

‘Yep.’

The third crate gave us another 30 boxes of Krugerrands. Another quarter of a million US Dollars.

‘Three more crates,’ he said. ‘Want to guess what’s in them?’

‘Clown hats,’ I said. ‘I’m going with clown hats and party streamers.’

Oliver opened the fourth crate. There were neither clown hats nor party streamers.

‘More drugs,’ he said, looking at the bags of white powder.

‘I’m going to guess that a certain senior detective has been a little bit dirty,’ I said. I looked back at Damian. He wasn’t enjoying this game. I should do something about his wounds, I thought.

‘Alright, Oliver, open that one.’ I pointed at the penultimate crate.

It contained a dozen semi-automatic pistols and a few hundred rounds of ammunition. Currency or protection? Both, maybe.

The last crate contained books. Accounting ledgers.

I sat back against the bulkhead and looked around the cabin.

‘So, we’ve got about half a million in gold coins, maybe five million in cocaine, a good stock of guns and ammo and a pile of ledgers.’

'Yeah, that's about the size of it,' said Oliver.

'Do you want to guess which crate is the most valuable?'

'The drugs,' he answered.

'No, I'm guessing it's the ledgers. Isn't that right, Damian?'

He was starting to look very pale.

'Why?' asked Oliver.

'In his former life, Johannes was an accountant. My guess is those ledgers contain a record of every item they've moved since they started this little scheme.'

I looked at Damian again. His cloudy eyes briefly met mine, then flicked away. I picked up a ledger at random, opened it part-way through and read about the cargoes they had moved. I read where they were moved from, where they went, who the buyer was, how much they paid, and - in this instance - how many children were in the cargo.

I made a decision. Oliver and I loaded the mountain, putting him next to the now unconscious Damian.

Three hours later, as dusk was beginning to settle around the airfield, I landed the Piaggio and taxied back behind the large hangar.

We unloaded the remaining three crates into Oliver's SUV. I patted the Piaggio's fuselage and silently thanked her for giving me a wonderful flight.

'You want one, Princess?'

'She's lovely,' I said. 'And a dream to fly but what would I do with something as beautiful as this?'

'Maybe dump rubbish far out at sea?'

'I won't be doing this again,' I said. 'Are you OK with driving Damian's truck?'

'No problem.'

'I'll drive yours. We'll rendezvous at the quarry we flew

over. Then, we clean, set fire to and push the burning Ranger into the quarry. But first, I'm going to make an anonymous call to the police about an abandoned truck.'

'And afterwards, back to the hotel for that meal we promised ourselves, right?'

'Right,' I said. 'A nice meal followed by an evening of slow relaxation.'

He grinned at me.

Chapter 41: Laura

The next day, Nala came to the hotel just before lunch. Despite the expensive outfit and well-tended hair, she looked a mess. Her bloodshot, shadowed eyes screamed sleeplessness.

'The police say they've found Dad's truck,' she said.

'Oh?' Oliver and I said at the same time.

'It's at some remote place outside Cape Town, on top of a mountain,' she said.

'But no sign of your father?' I asked.

'They are drafting in a team to look for him. They've asked me to go along.'

I nodded.

'I wondered...' she continued. 'I wondered if you would come too? I've got no one else to ask. Somebody to talk to who isn't a police officer would be... nice.'

'I've got an appointment with the US Consulate in an hour,' I lied. 'How about you go with Oliver and I'll come as soon as I've finished here?'

Oliver looked pleased but Nala looked nervous.

'Of course,' I continued quickly. 'If you are happy to wait until I'm done, we could all go together?'

She looked from me to Oliver a few times while she thought it over.

'No, I'd be happy to go with him. Perhaps you could drive?' she suggested.

'Sure,' said Oliver, being just a big, dumb male.

Minutes after they had left, I got on the phone and rented a shipping container. Then, I phoned some shipping agents. On the fifth call, I found an agent who had an aircraft engine that needed moving to the UK. They agreed to do the paperwork, and would collect the two crates I wanted moved. We shook metaphorical hands on the deal.

I changed into practical clothes and drove to the nearest shopping mall where I bought enough food for a troop of hungry people. Then, I followed Nala's directions to the place her father's car had been found.

At the top of the mountain, parked outside a fenced enclosure, was a marked police car, Oliver's SUV, a battered truck and a Land Rover. The writing on the Land Rover declared it belonged to the Mountain Club of South Africa.

Nala sat on a low wall near the battered truck, a female police officer next to her. Oliver was talking to another police officer and three people in climbing gear.

I parked up and walked over to Nala.

'No news yet,' she said. 'The MCSA Rescue Team are about to start looking on the mountainside.'

'Do they have any tracks they're going to follow?' I asked.

She shook her head.

'Too early. Once they go over the side, they will look for

fresh debris or broken branches.'

'This is definitely his car?' I asked.

'It is. His phone isn't in it but his gun is.'

She kept her gaze lowered. She already knew he was dead. Oliver walked over.

'The MCSA team are experienced people,' he said. 'They know these mountains and this is one they train on. They have arranged for a chopper with thermal imaging to come over and they're about to put a team over the side.'

'I've brought plenty of food and drink,' I said. 'It's in the back of my car. Tell them to help themselves if they want anything.'

'Smart thinking,' said Oliver as he walked over to tell them.

'Is there anything I can get for you?' I asked Nala.

She shook her head. I could see she wasn't taking this well, but this was the best place for her to be.

'I've got a couple of rugs in the car,' I said. 'If it gets chilly later, you should take one and wrap up.'

'You didn't have to go to all this trouble but thank you.'

I didn't know what to say. She was going to fall apart when they found Johannes' body. I turned and watched a member of the MCSA team clip her harness onto a safety line, climb onto the low wall and scale down the steep mountainside into the heavy undergrowth.

I turned back to Nala.

'How did they find his truck? A team come up to work on the antenna?'

She shook her head.

'Apparently the Cape police got a call last night. They don't know who it was but the caller said there was an abandoned truck up here.'

‘Could have been a climber or a mountain biker, I guess,’ I said.

‘Maybe.’ She didn’t care. She just wanted him back.

‘Chopper’s twenty minutes out,’ Oliver called.

I felt bad knowing she was pinning so much hope on him being found. I hadn’t liked the man. I hated what he had done, but Nala didn’t deserve to be punished for the sins of her father.

Another MCSA crew member arrived so they doubled their search by stringing another climber onto the mountainside. A crackle of radio communications announced the arrival of the helicopter. The chopper crew hooked up with the police officers and the MCSA team, then flew a search grid around the mountain.

After an hour, the helicopter’s thermal imaging equipment had found a pair of Ibex, a small herd of fallow deer and no humans.

The light was beginning to fade when one of the police officers came over. She said the helicopter had to return to base and it wouldn’t be long before the mountain rescue teams called it a day.

Nala looked devastated.

‘Can’t they work through the night?’ she asked.

The police officer explained that, because the severe incline was covered with thorny brush, trees and thick vegetation, working on the mountain in the dark was too dangerous. She said the MCSA teams would be back at first light.

The radio crackled as one of the rescue team said they were coming back up. The other MCSA members in the car park ran over to help. Two of the team pulled a searchlight from the back of the Land Rover and lit up the mountainside when I realised, they hadn't said they were coming up.

They had found him.

Chapter 42: Laura

Eventually, we took Nala home. She had wanted to stay on top of the mountain but the police said it was going to be several hours before they took the body to the mortuary. Formal identification of the deceased would take place tomorrow. Those words - 'body', 'mortuary', 'formal identification of the deceased' - hit her hard. She collapsed into Oliver's arms. He swept her up and gently put her in the back seat of the car.

It was pitch black when we arrived at the bungalow and lights came on as we approached the house.

'Sensors,' she said. 'They switch on when they detect movement.'

She unlocked the side door and led us into the kitchen.

'I'll fix us something,' said Oliver.

I was going to object but I left him to it. He was probably speaking for himself more than he was for Nala and me.

I asked where her bedroom was and she led me down a passage to a large, beautiful room. I found the en-suite, switched on the shower and gently told her to get ready for bed. She moved like a robot, going through the motions. She peeled her dress off, carefully hanging it in a huge wardrobe, and walked into the bathroom. I went back to the kitchen.

Oliver was making omelettes. There were three glasses of amber liquid beside the cooker.

'She needs a tranquiliser,' he said. 'I found some scotch in the cupboard. It'll do for now.'

I appreciated what he was doing for her. He owed this young woman nothing but here he was, trying to smooth the bumps out for her. Oliver continued to surprise me.

'Serious question: are we leaving her here tonight?'

'No,' he answered without taking time to consider. 'We'll pitch up here. It's a large house. There'll be space for us here. There's enough food to feed a squad and the very last thing we're going to do is leave her alone in the house tonight.'

'OK.'

'Is that it? No argument?' he asked.

'I've lost people close to me. In those times, the company of someone who cared for me would have stopped me from making the biggest mistake of my life,' I said. 'We're staying for her. Whatever she needs, she gets.'

He tended the omelette, then looked at me.

'You surprise me sometimes.'

'I was just thinking the same thing about you,' I said.

'Sometimes, you're all Captain Hardass. You've been there, done everything and can do it three times better than anyone else, and do it all with a blindfold on. You can kill a person with just a look…'

'Yes?' I questioned with a touch of threat in my voice.

'Then, you show a depth of feeling that nobody would have believed. You're tender and defenceless and vulnerable and lonely and…' He let the sentence trail off.

'Do not tell anyone about this,' I said.

'No, ma'am,' he said as he waved the spatula in a half-hearted salute.

'Do not tell anyone about what?' asked Nala as she walked into the kitchen.

'I'm giving Oliver orders not to tell anyone that I don't like mushrooms,' I said.

'Why don't you like mushrooms? she asked.

'Because she's not a fun guy to be around,' said Oliver.

She looked from me to him and back again.

'It's an old army joke,' I said.

'You were in the army?'

'Yes,' we both confirmed.

Oliver put a plate in front of Nala and slid one of the half-full glasses towards her.

'You need to eat this,' he said. 'You need to drink that, and then you need to go to bed.'

She stared at the plate for a moment, said she wasn't hungry, and started to eat. After a couple of mouthfuls, she smiled.

'This is really good!'

'Naturally,' Oliver said.

'Where did you learn to cook?'

'Mostly Iraq,' he said.

'Iraq?'

'And a little bit in Tennessee.'

'Were you posted there? In the army? Tennessee?' she asked.

'No. I had a bad holiday there. The food was awful so I learned to cook it myself.'

'Don't get him started, Nala,' I said. 'It's one short step from his worst holiday to his ex-wife.'

'You have an ex-wife?'

'I'm looking to fill the number two slot, if you're interested?'

'Oliver, leave the poor girl alone,' I said. 'You've already dazzled her with your culinary skills. She's going to down that half-glass of whiskey and then we'll put her bed. She doesn't need your weird sense of humour.'

I turned to Nala.

'Is it alright if we stay the night? We can all go into Cape Town in the morning.'

She looked relieved.

'Yes, please. I would like that. I'll make up the spare bedroom.'

'Just tell me where it is and where to find the bed linen,' I said.

'Third door on the left, down the main passageway. Clean sheets are in the wardrobe.'

It took five minutes to make up the bed and find some clean towels. Back in the kitchen, the plates had been cleared, Oliver was washing up and Nala was staring into space. I persuaded her into her bedroom and left her to it.

'You,' I said to Oliver. 'Shower, then bed.'

'Feeling frisky?'

'Not in someone else's house, not under these circumstances. I'm beat. It's been a busy couple of days and I need some sleep.'

He stretched his arms over his head, his impressive muscles rippling beneath his shirt.

'No argument from me, Princess.'

An hour later, we were both fast asleep.

Chapter 43: Laura

After a light breakfast, the three of us headed back to Cape Town. Along the way, I asked a question that had been bothering me.

'Who looks after the dog?'

'What dog?'

'When we came to see your father, there was a dog barking.'

'Oh,' she said. 'It's not real. It's a device wired in to the doorbell. Dad got it years ago.'

'I didn't have your father down as a gadget guy,' I said.

'He is... He *was* sometimes. He used to pick up little gadgets that caught his eye when he went to wine fairs. He didn't really leave the farm for much else.'

I made a mental note to check the farm laptop for Bluetooth devices.

'That's neat,' I said. 'Did he have many other little gadgets in the house?'

'You mean apart from the hidden camera in the guest bedroom?'

I looked at her tired face in the mirror.

'You're rubbish at kidding,' I said.

'Dad always said I was no good at cards,' she agreed.

'It wouldn't have seen much,' said Oliver. 'Princess fell asleep immediately and I went for a naked walk around the house.'

Nala looked at him sharply.

'No. You're joking,' she said.

'I doubt it,' I chimed in. 'But, if your dad has any more gadgets around the house, you'd be able to check.'

'Just the fake dog,' she said but, after a pause, 'There are a few burglar alarms around the farm, though.'

'We haven't seen the farm. Is it large?'

'Eighty-five hectares.'

'So, about 210 acres?' I asked.

'That's right.'

'Could you show us around before we leave South Africa?' I asked.

'When are you going?'

'End of next week,' Oliver said.

She paused before saying, 'It's strange to say this but I'm going to miss you.'

Something in her defencelessness pulled at me. She was, in some ways, still a child. The product of an over-protective parent? Yes, but she lacked the push, the ambition to get out on her own.

'Would you like to have dinner with us?' I asked. 'At the hotel, this evening?'

She looked out of the window at the passing countryside for a few moments.

'That's a nice offer. Can I think about it?'

'Of course,' I replied.

We lapsed into a contemplative silence until we pulled up outside the Western Cape Forensic Pathology Laboratory building on the Tygerberg Hospital campus.

The receptionist took Nala's details, dealt with us sympathetically and showed us to a small waiting room. A few minutes later, a man in a white coat took us into a viewing area where the shape of a body lay beneath a green sheet on a gurney. He asked if Nala was ready to identify the deceased.

She said she was.

He took hold of the sheet and drew it down to the body's

chest, exposing his head and shoulders. It was definitely Johannes.

Nala's head dropped but she remained silent.

The mortuary attendant asked if she could identify the deceased.

Nala almost inaudibly uttered 'yes' but that was enough for the attendant.

The sheet was drawn over Johannes and the attendant led us back to reception.

As we walked, Nala asked what would happen next. The mortuary attendant explained that there would be an autopsy to determine the cause of death. After the autopsy, the medical examiner would sign a death notification form which would enable the body to be released for burial.

She took it all in, showing little emotion but, as soon as we were back in the car, she broke down into deep, heaving sobs.

'Hotel?' asked Oliver.

'I think we should go back to the farm,' I said as I slid into the back seat next to Nala. I put my arm around her and hugged her as she cried into my shoulder.

Eventually, her sobs subsided but she stayed tucked against my shoulder. She may have slept some of the way home but she was awake when we pulled up to the bungalow.

We spent an hour going through the winery paperwork and scrolling through files on the computer. Unsurprisingly, everything was neatly organised. Nala found the family solicitor's details so she called them and arranged an appointment.

Oliver brought in drinks and sandwiches. Nala said she wasn't hungry but she nibbled at some crusts. I thought about a change of scenery; sitting in the house like this wasn't doing her any good.

'How about you show us around the farm?' I asked.

She considered it for a moment then agreed.

We got in Nala's 4x4 and she drove us further into the mountains before pulling over beside a lake.

'This is our main water supply,' she said. 'It's on the highest point of the farm. We use a network of pipes which we can turn on and off. That controls which parts of the farm get water.'

'Like the acequia system the Moors used in North Africa and Spain?' I asked.

'The Romans invented it but yes, it's essentially the same. Our farm manager used to switch the water flow around before he died but Dad had it automated. The switches are powered by solar.'

'That's neat,' said Oliver. 'Where does the lake get its water from?'

'There are three mountain springs that feed it. We don't know where they originate, maybe not even in the Western Cape.'

'And those barns,' I asked, pointing at three of the large, distant structures. 'What do you use them for?'

'That one.' She pointed out. 'That's where the harvested grapes are washed, de-stemmed and pressed. That one.' She pointed further down the mountain. 'Is where the juice is stored to ferment.'

'And that one?' I asked, pointing to the most distant, most southerly building on the farm.

'That's where we used to bottle the wine after fermentation but the bottling plant was an expensive overhead so we send the wine away for bottling now.'

'Why do you use separate buildings?' asked Oliver.

'We didn't intend to. It's how the winery has grown up. We used to do everything in one building but, as we expanded, we built the new barns.'

It was an impressive sight. Thousands of rows of well-tended vines stretched down the hillside with the bungalow nestled in a sheltered dip, away from the centre of the farm. This hadn't happened overnight; it had taken decades of effort and management to make the winery into a prosperous business.

Chapter 44: Laura

It was late afternoon when we said goodbye. I said we needed to get back to the hotel to change our clothes as Oliver was starting to smell. He looked offended but Nala laughed.

We bumped our way down the track, turned at the unused barn on the junction and drove on down the hill.

'Can you pull over in that gateway?'

'I don't really smell. Right?'

'Right,' I said, smiling.

He pulled over.

'What's up?'

'I've got an itch that needs scratching,' I answered then quickly said, 'Not that kind of itch. Come for a walk.'

Oliver got out.

'Talk to me,' he said.

'We're going over there,' I pointed at the distant barn on the edge of a mountain rise, a little over 2 kilometres through the field.

Oliver squinted into the distance; the shadows were growing long in the setting sun.

'That's the bottling plant?'

'The former bottling plant but yes, that's it,' I answered.

'You're going to make me walk a couple of klicks through rows of grape vines just to look at an old bottling plant?'

'No, Oliver,' I explained patiently. 'I'm asking you to walk a couple of kilometres through rows of grape vines just to look at an old barn.'

'You reckon it's where stuff was stored? Before it was flown out?'

'Seems logical,' I said.

'OK, Princess. Lead us to the barn of mystery and adventure.'

'Did you watch too much Scooby Doo when you were a child?'

'Don't diss the Scooby Doo,' he retorted.

'Come on, Shaggy. I'll race you.'

I set off at a brisk jog up the line of grape vines but Oliver had other ideas and sprinted past me. I stepped on the gas but he stopped short of the barn and held his hand up. I pulled up in the row next to him.

'See this pole?' he asked, pointing to a scaffolding pole sticking up about 3 metres.

'Well, duh.'

'It had something attached to it, just a little way above the ground.'

Although they were coated with rust, the marks on the metal pole were easy to see. Oliver stepped sideways through a couple of rows of vines until he came to another upright pole.

'This one's the same,' he called over as he stepped over another couple of rows. 'There's another here.'

'These poles, they're not attached to the wirework that holds the vines in place but could they have been? Maybe when they were setting up the rows?'

'Yeah, could be,' he conceded. 'But those marks are at the right height for some tripwires.' He thought about it for a couple of moments. 'But why would you have tripwires in the middle of a vineyard?'

I shrugged.

'It's probably nothing,' he said. 'Let's get to the barn before it gets dark.'

We walked the rest of the way. The barn stood in a small clearing, set apart from the rows of vines. It looked like it was made out of steel panels bolted onto a metal frame. The roof was the standard corrugated tin but there were solar panels over the top. Three tracks approached the barn: the one we'd parked at the end of, another that led further down the mountain and a third that looked like it might go back to the bungalow.

'Quick check?' I asked.

'You're the boss, Boss.'

'I thought I was Princess?'

'Princesses can't be the boss?'

'Yes, they can,' I said. 'Don't mess with boss Princesses. Meet back here. I'll go left.'

I circled the barn clockwise; Oliver went anti-clockwise. We passed each other on the far side and met up back where we'd started. We compared what we'd seen.

'Double door on the west side,' he said. 'Four external locking points.'

'Check.'

'No tyre tracks. No signs of recent occupation. No signs of recent access.'

'Check.'

'Solar all over the roof, cable ducting into the barn in two ingress points.'

'Check.'

'What you got?'

'No windows. No secondary door. A small whip antenna at the top of the east side.'

'Check.'

'The barn is set on a concrete footing. Can't tell how thick but it looks substantial.'

'Check.'

I paused.

'Anything else?' he asked.

'The track that goes down the mountain.'

'What about it?'

'It's wrong,' I said.

'How so?'

'From what Nala said, that track doesn't go anywhere useful.'

'Maybe it's a drainage thing? A soakaway?' he pondered.

'Why would you level out a track for that? You'd put a backhoe in here and trench out downhill. You're not going to need to drive down it ever again so building a track is just a waste of money and land.'

'You may have a point,' he said thoughtfully.

'Well… On the one hand, some people like wasting money.'

'Yeah, right,' he said disbelievingly.

'On the other hand, I don't believe Johannes is that kind of person. Let's check the track out.'

'What about the barn?' he asked.

'It's not going anywhere. We'll be back before dark.'

Chapter 45: Laura

The track ran down a steep incline to a large, deep hollow where it came to a dead end.

'And this is where the trail ends, pardner,' Oliver said in a bad Texan drawl.

I didn't answer straight away. I walked a little way around the hollow, then clambered and skidded down the steep incline onto the bottom, and walked around some more. It hadn't been carved out by man or, if it had, it had been done thousands of years ago but there were signs of activity more recent than that.

'Some of these rocks have been scraped,' I called up to him.

'By tools, you mean?'

'Not shovels and pickaxes. Something big. A digger, maybe? Not recently because the scrapes are weathered but the edges aren't rounded off, so within the last fifty years.'

'You're a geologist now?'

'Yes, I am.'

'Want me to come down there?'

'No need, I'm coming back,' I said, and began the steep climb up.

I was almost at the top when Oliver reached down to give

me a hand up. Either he was being helpful or he was trying to sneak a look down my blouse because the horny teenager is never far below Oliver's surface. He stretched out his hand, bent over and rolled forward down the incline. If I hadn't stepped aside, he would have bowled me over.

I heard the distant bang of a gunshot as Oliver tumbled towards the bottom. Not a shotgun, but not a military-grade weapon; the lag in the sound of the shot told me the bullet was from a small calibre subsonic rifle, and had been fired some distance away.

I stumbled to the bottom of the hollow and checked Oliver's crumpled form. He had a hole in the back of his right shoulder. There was no exit wound in either his chest or his side so the bullet was still inside him. That's OK.

I took my jacket off, rolled it up tight and stuffed it beneath his shirt against the entry wound. Stem the bleeding first, deal with the bullet later.

He was conscious, dazed but not looking like he was in too much pain.

'Keep still. The position you're in is the most comfortable for you right now.'

I had blood on my hands which I smeared across the front of my blouse. I hated doing it but surviving is more important than a fitted blouse.

'Look at me,' I said quietly but urgently. 'Oliver, look at me! It's important. I'm going to lie here. I need you to keep perfectly still. Close your eyes and pretend you're dead. Whoever shot you will get here in a minute. They won't waste another bullet on you if they think you're already dead. Do you understand? Oliver!'

He exhaled slowly. Maybe he had a punctured lung or

maybe the bullet was inside his lung. He needed medical treatment, fast.

'Hey, big dog. I'll get you to an ER. You'll be loaded up on happy stuff and won't remember the pain. You've got a new scar you can brag to your next wife about. Just keep still and play possum. Understand?'

'Princess?'

'Be dead, Oliver. Be dead and stay alive.'

'It hurts.'

'I'll kiss it better in a few days but, right now, be-'

Footsteps crunched on the gravel. Someone was walking towards the hollow.

I lay on my back, my right arm twisted behind me, my left arm at an awkward angle over my head.

A handful of loose stones tumbled down the side of the hollow. They were standing on the top looking down. In the early evening gloom, they saw Oliver, bloody and unconscious, possibly dead. Me, unconscious with maybe a broken arm and some bleeding from a chest injury.

They didn't move. The evening air was still and silent. Nothing moved. Nobody moved. I didn't breathe. I hoped Oliver wasn't breathing. Could they even see us breathing from up there?

Keep still, Oliver. I'll feed you and take you to bed as soon as we're through this. Just don't breathe now.

Some more stones fell on us and I heard the crunch of footsteps as they skidded down the incline.

Do. Not. Breathe.

They edged closer. Closer. Behind my closed eyes, the pain of not breathing was turning my world red when a foot kicked me in the ribs.

No breath to breathe with, lungs not working in or out. I moaned in pain but kept it low.

I heard the cocking of a rifle so I groaned again and threw up the handful of soil from my left hand. As I threw it, I pulled my right hand out from behind my back, sighted through squinted eyes and pulled the trigger of Johannes' Vektor twice.

There was no look of surprise on her face because my second shot removed most of the front of her head. The first shot was into her chest.

At this close distance, the chest shot from a 9mm pistol would have penetrated thin steel. It would go right through a human's chest, internal organs, spine and out into the countryside. The headshot threw her head violently backwards.

I unsquinted my eyes and watched the body fall to the ground. Silver dress, matching watch and necklace and an incongruous pair of clumpy walking boots.

Nala had come to stop us from looking for something, we'd got too close to it, and now I knew what it was. I knew what we were laying on.

I shivered and it wasn't from the cold.

Chapter 46: Laura

The air ambulance landed next to the hollow, throwing up dust and leaves and dirt. The paramedics attached a gurney to a rope and pulley device, lowering it down. Oliver wasn't talking much but he was awake and wheezing. When the medics had treated him as best they could and loaded him onto the gurney, they raised him up to the helicopter. They came back to help me and I tried to tell them I looked worse than I was, but in the far distance I could see the red, white and blue flashing lights of the South African Police. I decided to let them interrogate me later, and climbed into the helicopter.

We landed on a helipad at the Christiaan Barnard Memorial Hospital in Cape Town where we were rushed into an Emergency and Trauma Care triage unit. A specialist asked Oliver some questions while he checked him over before stepping back and telling the nurse to prep for theatre. Oliver was wheeled away. The clinician took one look at the state of me and asked if I'd been shot too. I said I was mostly wearing Oliver's blood but he ordered a nurse to take me to a treatment room, examine me carefully and clean me up.

While I was being examined, I heard voices outside the treatment room. The local police had arrived and wanted to know where the casualties had got to. Whoever the police were talking to was adamant that neither Oliver nor I were going to be disturbed.

After I'd been cleaned up, I was given a hospital gown to wear. My clothes were bundled into a bag, too ruined to put back on. A nurse came to say that Oliver was being prepped for surgery. She asked if I wanted to see him and I said yes

The nurse went out and came back with a wheelchair.

The police tried to get in my face when I was wheeled out of the treatment room but the nurse who was wheeling me wasn't taking any crap. We skittled through them and into the surgical room where Oliver was on a gurney, attached to a drip and a bunch of monitoring devices.

'Slacking again?' I asked him.

He wheezed his breathy response.

'You've been on my case so much I'm enjoying the peace and quiet.'

'And now I'm here,' I said.

'And now you're here,' he repeated. 'I'm glad. How come you get wheels and I get a bed?'

'Because you're a slacker and I've got places to go and people to see,' I said.

'Ah.' He knew what I meant. He coughed and the devices beeped.

'Apparently, I have gained a little weight,' he said.

'Yeah, I saw the entry and couldn't find the exit. Essentially, you're trying to sneak out of South Africa with some undeclared material.'

'That's one way of looking at it.'

The clinician came back in, dressed for business.

'We're going to take you away now, Oliver,' he said. 'You'll be able to share some more of your impressive humour later.'

'Oh, God. He's been working through his jokes?'

'He has,' said the nurse who had wheeled me in.

'I'm so very sorry,' I said.

I watched them wheel him into the operating theatre next door.

'What's his prognosis?' I asked the clinician.

'Pretty good. He's fit and healthy. The bullet's passed into his right lung. We'll get in, remove it, drain any fluid and then patch his lung. I've seen a few gunshot wounds; this one hasn't caused much internal damage.'

'Thanks for the update. Will I be allowed to stay here until he regains consciousness?'

He looked towards the door behind me.

'That mostly depends on the police. As far as hospital policy goes, we can find space for you to stay but the police want to ask questions and they may not want to do that here.'

I said I understood and I did. No hospital is the right place for a police interrogation.

He turned and walked into the operating theatre. The nurse opened the curtain and wheeled me back into the treatment room where three police officers were waiting for me.

Chapter 47: Laura

The police wanted to take me to a police station but I dug my feet in. I wasn't going anywhere until Oliver was out of surgery and had regained consciousness. They insisted. I told them to stuff it. I said I'd give them some time now at the hospital and that I'd go down to the station as soon as Oliver was awake and talking. I wasn't going to move from his side until he called me 'Princess' again.

They said they could remove me by force if I didn't cooperate. I said I wouldn't cooperate if they removed me by force.

Stalemate.

The younger of the uniformed officers (who looked barely old enough to be out of school) excused herself from the room while the senior detective tried to browbeat me into going to the station.

I'd just told him he could stick his head up a dead bear's bum when the young constable came back in. She asked the detective to step outside.

A few moments later, they returned.

'Constable Nkosi has found an administrator's office on the first floor we can use. Can we have a conversation in there?'

'Yes, that would be most acceptable,' I said and I flashed the constable a smile of thanks. 'Can we let the ER staff know where I will be, in case there's any change in Oliver's status?'

'I will do that for you,' she said.

I thanked her again as an orderly wheeled me to the administrator's office.

It wasn't much of an office; I've used larger public toilets but we all squeezed in and closed the door.

'Now then, Miss Guerra,' the senior detective said. 'Tell me all about it.'

So, I did. Well, I left out a couple of things. I started with Johannes going missing, Nala coming to the hotel, Oliver looking at Johannes' laptop, which led us to Damian. This drew a sharp breath around the room.

One of the uniformed police officers excused himself.

I talked about how we followed Damian which led to the discovery of crates in the hangar at the flying club. I swerved around the truth here. I told them about my discovery of the ledgers and the one book I managed to look at before Damian and his armed sidekick made their getaway with the crates of loot.

Then, I told them about walking across the field to the barn, going down to the hollow and Oliver getting shot.

The detective asked a lot of questions about that. I said Nala had dropped the pistol down the side of the hollow while she was fumbling with the rifle. I'd picked up the gun and shot her with it. He nodded as he already knew the gun

I'd used was registered to Johannes.

I knew I would have to repeat the story when they got me to a police station. I also knew I'd have to run Oliver through this shortened version of the truth but I didn't think he'd have a problem with it. The police were taking notes and the recorder they'd put on the desk was catching everything. We would need to have our script down pat.

I asked if we could take a break.

The detective leaned over the desk and fixed me with a stare.

'I have to say, Miss Guerra, you seem remarkably calm after the ordeal you've been through.'

I gave him a blank stare.

'Your friend was shot. You've been shot at. You even returned fire with, I have to say, remarkable accuracy.'

'It's been more active than a typical day,' I conceded.

'And your accuracy with a gun?'

'Beginner's luck,' I said.

He grunted.

'Constable Nkosi will stay with you for the time being. If you remember anything else, please let her know.'

'I will,' I said.

'And, as soon as your friend is conscious, I will need to see you at the police station.'

'Will I be allowed to go to the hotel to freshen up and change into clothes first?' I asked, indicating the hospital gown I was still wearing.

'Yes, of course,' he answered.

'And my phone. I need my phone, please. I've got to tell people about Oliver being shot.'

'I'll get that for you,' said Constable Nkosi.

I thanked her.

As soon as I had my phone, I'd be able to send a message to Oliver to give him the shortened version of the story. All I had to do was make sure he read it before he talked to the police.

Satisfied that they had no more questions to ask me, I was wheeled back down to the ER waiting room.

Constable Nkosi sat beside me but we didn't talk much.

Chapter 48: Laura

Two hours after Oliver was wheeled into surgery, the surgeon came into the waiting room. She pulled a chair round to face me, sat down and looked me steadily in the eye. Constable Nkosi leaned in to catch every word.

'The extraction was successful. He had one small tear where the bullet entered his lung but there was no other lung damage. We've patched the hole; I would expect that to heal rapidly. There wasn't much fluid in either of his lungs, so we decided against putting a chest drain in. We cleaned out some small fragments; they were nothing major, probably caused by the bullet before it settled into his lung.

'You can go in and see him but he won't make much sense.'

'Yes, please,' I said.

'I think your friend has an excellent prognosis. We will keep him in intensive care for a few days. After that, he can go on to a general ward.'

'How long do you think he'll have to remain here?'

She looked thoughtful for a few moments.

'I don't want to say right now. Things might go well; things might not go entirely smoothly. We humans aren't machines,' she said.

'I understand, it's just that he was due to start a new job in a few weeks.'

'Ah. Is it a physically demanding job?'

I thought of Oliver's work for Whiteland Security.

'Occasionally, yes.'

'In that case, I would warn his employer of the possibility that he may not be able to start work for a few months.'

'A few *months*?'

'Just to be safe, yes,' she said.

'What about flights?' I asked.

'Again, this depends on his recovery but let's say no sooner than six weeks. It may be longer but it's unlikely to be quicker.'

I had thought of Oliver as being a powerful man, strong as an ox. This diagnosis from the surgeon was making me think twice.

'Do you have any questions for me?' she asked.

'No. I think I've got what I need for now. Can I see him, please?'

'Of course. Just remember what I said about him not making much sense for a while.'

I tried a smile.

'In some ways, doctor, that's not too different from normal.'

She smiled back, signalled a porter to wheel me into the intensive care unit and walked beside me. Constable Nkosi followed at a respectful distance.

Oliver lay in a bay, the sheet around his bed space open. Three monitors on the far side beeped quietly and flashed on-screen messages in a soothing shade of blue. He wore a surgical gown and was connected to a ventilator.

'We will remove the ventilator within the hour. He has good strong lungs, this is just a precaution.'

'I understand,' I said.

'Hey, big dog,' I said as I took his hand in mine. 'You have to promise me you aren't going to annoy the nurses, OK?'

He grunted softly.

'I'm going back to the hotel to pack some things and bring them back. Will you be here in an hour?'

He squeezed my hand. That was good enough.

'I'll be back soon. You just lie there and make the place look untidy, OK?'

He squeezed my hand again.

I looked at the surgeon.

'Thank you. This big oaf means something to me. I appreciate what you've done for us.'

When I said the word 'oaf', Oliver squeezed my hand. Two squeezes, a long hold, one squeeze, a pause, two squeezes, a long hold.

I looked at his eyes. They were not entirely focussed but he'd just morse coded F U at me. He was telling me he was OK.

The wave of relief almost made me feel dizzy.

Chapter 49: Laura

I took a taxi back to the hotel, Constable Nkosi sat in the back with me. She said she'd wait in the lounge while I got changed. I asked if she'd eaten lately, discovered she hadn't, so I ordered her a coffee, a sandwich and some cake.

In the suite, I stripped off and hit the bathroom. I ran the hottest shower and stood beneath the spray, letting the scorching water pound against me while I got my thoughts together.

I was angry. Angry at what had happened to Oliver. Angry that it had been Nala who shot him and angry that we'd blundered around like a pair of amateurs. The former bottling plant obviously had some kind of electronic protection.

I was furious. I'm supposed to be a pro. Hell, Oliver is supposed to be a pro but we were both caught out and that made me bloody angry. There was no-one I could take it out on. That made me angry too.

I stayed in the shower, trying to make the worst of my rage evaporate but, when I got out, there was still a hard, bitter lump of anger deep inside my stomach. I needed to get rid of it.

I put on my sweats and took the elevator to the basement gym. I worked hard on the rowing machine until I couldn't take any more. Then, I jumped on the exercise bike, turned the resistance up and pushed myself until my legs felt like rubber. I hit the weights press until I couldn't press any more. I looked at the cable machine but I had nothing left to give: I'd worn myself out too quickly.

Feeling like I was used up, I went back to our suite where I had another shower and put on fresh clothes. Then, I packed some things for Oliver in one rucksack, put my washbag, clean underwear and spare t-shirt in another.

On wobbly legs, I made my way back downstairs. I called for Constable Nkosi in the lounge while the hotel got us a taxi.

'What time did you start your shift?' I asked as we settled into the back seat.

'Eight o'clock,' she said.

'That was over twelve hours ago. Do you get overtime?'

Her face cracked in a huge grin.

'Better than overtime,' she said. 'I work a twelve-hour shift, but when I work over hours, I take my overtime in flexi. That way, I don't get taxed.'

I nodded my understanding; this was the most she'd said to me so far.

'That's shrewd. I like the way you think. How long have you been a police officer?'

'Eight months.'

'Do you enjoy it?'

'I do. It's my first real job and I'm learning a lot.'

She seemed bright and I felt she had a lot to contribute. I stifled a yawn.

'Sorry. It's been a long day,' I said.

'A lot has happened to you. And to your friend.'

'Yeah, he's had a hell of a day.'

'The surgeon was positive about his chances of recovery.'

'I think he's going to be fine.'

'And, after you've spoken with him, you'll come to the police station?'

'Yes, that's what I said. Your detective is going to have a lot to do when I finish talking. Are you on his staff?'

'No. I was on duty when the call came in. We were asked to send a female officer and I was the only one immediately available.'

'Ah, OK. Well, as I said, he's going to have a lot to do. I

should imagine things will be very busy tomorrow. There will be a lot of flexitime coming up.' I looked at her.

'I'll make sure I'm available to help.'

A brief smile passed between us and we lapsed into silence for the rest of the journey.

At the ER reception, I was asked to wait because the surgeon was seeing to Oliver. I got nervous and paced across the room.

Eventually, the surgeon and a nurse came out.

'Miss Guerra,' she said. 'You can go in and see him now. He seems to have the constitution of an ox. His breathing doesn't need any assistance so we've just removed the ventilator but we will continue monitoring him closely.'

Relief flooded through me.

'He was lightly sedated for the ventilator removal. He's still a little groggy but he can talk, if he's feeling up to it.'

'When will the police be able to interview him?' asked Constable Nkosi.

'I'll make that decision after I've seen him tomorrow morning,' said the surgeon. 'See me after nine o'clock.'

I didn't want to stand there while they had their conversation so I walked straight into Oliver's room. He was slightly propped up in bed, looking a little sleepy. The sheet was pulled back and there was a dressing on the right side of his ribs.

'How are you doing, big dog?'

He looked at me.

'Ruff.'

'Christ, the jokes in here are terrible.'

'Bella said they will get better with time.'

'And who the hell is Bella?'

'She's the nurse looking after me.'

'I need to have words with Bella.'

'Jealous?'

'Not at all, but her judgement on your sense of humour needs realigning.'

'Doctor!' he fake called out. 'This lady is bullying me.'

'Oh, shush. You need to check your phone when you can. I'm sure there are lots of messages for you.'

'My legion of fans, you mean?'

'Yeah, but it's probably the IRS asking when you can pay the money you owe.'

He groaned and flapped a hand.

'Got to be honest, Princess, my head hurts and my side hurts more.'

I put my hand on his arm.

'I'll leave you alone soon. You need to rest. The police want me downtown for a chat about who did what.'

'How long ago?' he asked.

'About five hours. You need to rest and I mean *sleep*, not chasing nurses all over the hospital.'

'What are you going to do?'

'I'll let Constable Nkosi take me downtown. Then, I'll come back here. The surgeon said I could stay so I'll doze in that chair while you sleep,' I pointed to the large chair in the corner beside his bed. 'The surgeon said she'll check you over at oh-nine-hundred so I'm staying until at least then.'

'You should go back to the hotel, get some sleep.'

'I will, sooner or later,' I said. 'First, you sleep. I'll go to the police station. I'll be back as soon as I I'm done there, OK?'

'OK.'

Chapter 50: Laura

Nkosi checked us in and I was directed to an interrogation suite. Inside was a CCTV camera and, set into a wall beside the sturdy-looking, metal desk, two microphones and recording equipment. The walls were a neutral shade of bland. None of the four chairs looked comfortable. There was a dark, glass panel set in another wall.

I took a seat.

A moment later, the two police officers walked in through the doorway opposite. Good cop and better cop; a sergeant detective and a uniformed lieutenant.

The detective put a portable recorder on the desk, switched it on, then flicked on the recording equipment set into the wall. He recited the date and time, his name and rank, and asked me for my name, which I gave him.

He said the purpose of the interview was to look into two shootings on land belonging to the Cape Heartland Wine Estate, Cape Town. The shootings occurred at approximately 17.10 the previous evening.

Then, the interview began.

We were half an hour into the session when the door opened and a new person in civilian clothes walked in. I guessed he was a senior police officer judging by the instant reactions from the officers in the room.

'Carry on,' he said. 'Pretend I'm not here.'

They couldn't pretend he wasn't there but, before they carried on with the interrogation, the detective announced to the recording equipment that Lieutenant General Philip Sorenson had entered the room.

Two hours later, we had covered everything up to Oliver

being loaded into the helicopter. The recording equipment was left running but we seemed to be taking a break. One of the detectives asked if I would like something to eat or drink and left the room to get me a glass of water and some fruit.

'Miss Guerra,' said the Lieutenant General. 'You seem to have been extraordinarily lucky with your shooting. That wasn't an easy shot to make from the bottom of the hollow, especially as you were lying on your back.'

The way he phrased it… It wasn't a question but his rising inflection made it seem like one. My choices were to be cute, be honest or to lie.

I chose cute.

'It's not the first time I've had my hand around a dangerous weapon.'

'Yes, quite.' I don't think he was impressed with my response. He went on. 'Can I ask you a question that may have been covered before I arrived?'

'Sure, why not?' I replied. After all, I'm not the one with stuff to hide… Apart from all of the omissions in my statement.

'We've heard that you made your way from your car across to the barn, a distance of about 2 kilometres, and then walked down the track and climbed into the hollow. What was it that drew your attention there?'

They'd been shocked at the revelation of Damian and the mountain's activities. Now, it was time to drop the really big bomb.

'I suspect there are a number of bodies buried in the hollow.'

'Really?' The Lieutenant General's composure didn't budge but the detective's mouth set in a firm line.

'Yes,' I said. 'At least one but likely to be more.'

'What makes you think this?'

'Something has been buried there. There are traces of heavy machinery on the rocks. The track doesn't go anywhere and Nala had already told us the barn near the hollow used to be a bottling plant,' I paused to take a deep breath. 'That's ridiculous. A bottling plant would need lorries to supply it with clean, empty bottles. It would need lorries to take away the full bottles to wherever they were going to be stored...'

He nodded, encouraging me to go on.

'Why would the bottling plant be in the middle of the crops? Why would the lorries need to drive across a track laid down through the middle of the grape vines?'

'But the dead bodies?' he asked.

'I think the bottling plant was where Johannes and Damian kept the things they were shipping out of the country before they got to the airfield. Sometimes, the things they were shipping out were people. Young children, probably homeless kids off the streets. I think their human cargo didn't always make it out of that barn alive. I suspect you'll find children's bodies in that hollow. I also think you'll find the body of the former farm manager there.'

'Why do you think that?' asked the Lieutenant General.

'I think the farm manager discovered something or perhaps he looked the right way at the wrong time. Maybe he was in on everything from the start and began to get greedy, but whatever happened, Nala said he had died. He wasn't replaced but Johannes automated what he could. Why?'

'To save money?' he said.

I gave him the blankest stare I had in me. He coughed to break the silence.

'I suggest you put a team on excavating that hollow,' I said.

'I think you'll find the answer to your question there.'

Chapter 51: Laura

Four hours later, I was allowed to head back to the hospital. The police supplied a chaperone/driver, a fresh-faced constable who looked about twelve years old. I don't suppose they had many spare officers sitting around not doing much at 05.00, especially after everything I'd dropped on them.

The young constable - Charles - followed me around like Nkosi the day before. We went straight to the intensive care ward.

Oliver was fast asleep so I settled into the chair and listened to the machines quietly monitoring his condition. A nurse came to record his vitals and I wondered why they still did that when the machines were recording the same information. She noted stuff down on a board at the end of his bed, turned to me and said he was doing fine. She didn't have to do that.

I gave her the warmest thank you I had in me then closed my eyes for a moment. The next thing I knew, it was full daylight outside.

'Hey, sleepyhead. I wondered when you were going to wake up.'

I stretched in the chair.

'I waited half the night for you to wake up and you beat me to it while I was taking a little doze? That's unjust.'

'Were you *just* having a little sleep?'

'Oliver, your gags are getting worse.'

'Hospitals have that effect on me.'

'Checked your phone?' I asked.

'Yes. Message received, loud and clear. I'm sure you'll tell me why?'

'I will.'

'Noted.'

'So, how are you feeling?'

'Bit spaced out. The pain meds are good but I feel like I've been kicked in the chest by a mule.'

'I guess getting a bullet in a lung would do that for you.'

'A nurse said they had to crack a couple of my ribs to get in there.'

'That'll definitely do it.'

'Thanks.'

'What for?'

'Getting me out of there. Getting me here. Making sure I got patched up.'

'It's nothing,' I really meant it.

The door opened and the surgeon, a couple of doctor types and two nurses filed in. The surgeon took the board from the end of the bed, ran her fingers down it then walked up to Oliver.

'So, Mister Jago, how are you feeling today?'

'To be honest, I feel great. I think I'm well enough to check out.'

She smiled at him.

'I doubt that but we'll take some blood in a minute, run some tests, see what's happening inside you. Have you been to the toilet yet?'

'Not really felt the need.'

'Call the nurse when you do and they'll help. I want you

to stay in bed until this afternoon. I'll make sure an orderly comes to help you into the chair. You may be starting to walk around by tomorrow but I would expect to see you sitting at your table for meals. The day after tomorrow, I'll schedule someone to help you walk down the corridor.'

'And back again?'

She smiled, as if dealing with an idiot.

'And back again.'

She consulted with her entourage, turned and said, 'See you tomorrow, Mister Jago,' before they swept out and on to the next patient.

'I like her style,' I said.

'Professional, no nonsense and no sense of humour?' he asked.

'Professional, no nonsense and no time for fools.'

'Hey! That hurt.'

'Shut up. Get well. Get out of here. In six weeks, you can fly. I'm taking you back to the UK where I can keep an eye on you. So, tell the people you've got lined up to see in the US you can't make it. Tell Whiteland Security you've been shot, you're in South Africa and you need to delay picking up the next contract.'

'Did you say you're taking me back to the UK?'

'Yes. I've got a couple of things to do over there. You're going to use the opportunity to rest and recuperate. If you don't, I'll have serious words with you.'

He leaned back into his pillow and sighed. 'Yes, ma'am.'

Charles walked in with the same two police officers who had interrogated me in the early hours.

'Mister Jago,' said the nice one. 'Your surgeon said we could ask you a few questions.'

‘We won’t be very long or very demanding,’ said the very nice one.

‘And I’m staying to make sure you don’t wear Oliver out,’ I said.

I don’t think they were impressed but I wasn’t going to give way and they could see the glint in my eye.

It took Oliver two hours to walk the police through the edited version of what they wanted to know. They switched off their recording equipment, put away their notebooks and packed up. The lead detective said they would be in touch if they needed anything more.

I gave them my best dead-eyed glare as they left the room.

Chapter 52: Laura

Six days later, it was Oliver’s first full day out of hospital. We were taking a slow, early evening walk around the hotel’s swimming pool when Constable Nkosi walked out of the lounge toward us.

‘I have been sent to ask if you could come to the police station this evening,’ she said to me.

‘Can you tell me why?’ I asked.

‘The Lieutenant General would like a meeting. He asked me to make it very clear this would be at your convenience but, if you could see him this evening, that would be better than tomorrow.’

I thought about whether I wanted to go or not. It was a polite invitation after all.

While I was mulling it over, I asked Nkosi a question.

‘How’s the flexitime coming along?’ Her grin grew even broader.

‘I am not supposed to tell you anything about the case but I don’t think it would be a problem to tell you I almost have enough flexi for an extra week off.’ She could barely contain her glee. Her infectious enthusiasm helped me make my decision.

‘OK, Nkosi. I’m in. Tell your man I could leave here in about half an hour?’

‘I will tell him but I will wait for you.’

‘Uhhh, I’d be happy to drive myself,’ I said.

She looked disappointed and then the penny dropped.

‘Of course. If you drive me to the police station, you’d have to wait around and then deliver me back here later?’

‘That is an excellent idea! I shall wait for you in the lounge.’ She turned and walked back the way she’d come.

‘What’s that about?’ asked Oliver.

‘She’s racking up flexitime instead of taking overtime. It adds to her leave entitlement and she doesn’t get taxed on it.’

He turned and looked at me.

‘So, you two have cooked up a little scheme to give her more paid time off?’

‘That’s about the size of it.’

‘That’s almost the perfect, truly victimless crime. I like it.’ He leaned over and kissed me. And then he kissed me again.

‘Oliver, there’s something wrong with your trousers.’ I pointedly looked down.

‘Goodness!’ he said. ‘How did that happen?’

‘I think I’ll have to investigate. Maybe I could have a look and see if we can recreate whatever it is later, when I get back from this meeting?’

'I like the sound of that. I don't want to disappoint but I don't think I'm up to our usual activities yet.'

'Don't you worry about that. I'll be gentle with you.'

I lifted his hand to my mouth, kissed it and held it tightly as we walked back to our suite.

Chapter 53: Laura

During the drive from the hotel, Nkosi betrayed no secrets about the investigation, but I did learn that her first name was Amahle. She remained enigmatic about everything else.

Surprisingly, she took me to the same non-descript building Damian and the mountain had worked in. Instead of an interview room, I was admitted behind the scenes where I was shown to a large meeting room.

Lieutenant General Sorenson was with a uniformed officer I hadn't met before, and the same two detectives who had interrogated me and Oliver.

'Miss Guerra, thank you for coming. Please, take a seat. Can I ask the constable to get you anything?'

I turned to Nkosi. 'Could I have a glass of water, please?'

She smiled, bobbed her head and walked to a nearby water cooler. Once my drink was placed in front of me, she left the room, closing the door behind her.

'How can I help you?' I asked.

'You understand that we had to verify everything you and your friend told the investigating officers?' he said.

'Of course,' I said.

'And I hope you would understand that we also had to

investigate you and Mister Jago?'

'I would expect as much.'

'It would seem from our enquiries that you and Mister Jago both have distinct but equally colourful histories.'

I took a sip of water. The lieutenant general went on.

'Mister Jago's profile was easy for us to piece together.' He picked up a sheet of paper and read from it. 'A highly experienced military operative, decorated for his service in the Middle East, North Africa, Central Europe and North Africa again.'

I shrugged.

'But you were more difficult to track down which led us to believe that Guerra isn't your real name.'

I opened my mouth to object but he waved me to silence and picked up another piece of paper.

'Oh, yes. Your passport, credit cards, driving licence and social security number are all correct, all issued through the correct channels. But our intelligence service couldn't track your history down. It's their opinion you have been given a new identity by the US Government. We managed to get the military service file attached to your Guerra identity from the Pentagon. We also got a notification of your work in Washington and England for the United States Defence Intelligence Analysis Centre. If we are to believe any of that is true.'

I took another sip of water and smiled.

'And then you pop up on our radar, making an enquiry about someone who seems to be a law-abiding South African civilian. That enquiry is routed through US intelligence channels? There are a number of things here that warrant deeper investigation.'

That was a bluff and everyone in the room knew it.

'A team of detectives was despatched to your hotel to bring you here for questioning but the Director of the NIA vouched for you. It subsequently transpires that those detectives had no legal reason or justification for even asking you the time of day.'

I play a mean hand of poker but I let this one go and grinned at him.

He plays good poker too. He kept a straight face.

'The next contact we have is when you call in that Mister Jago has been shot. We attend the scene and we discover Nala Marula's body. Finally, in your debriefing.' I noticed it wasn't an "interview" or an "interrogation". 'You tell us that a senior detective has been smuggling drugs, arms, and currency out of the country, and trafficking vulnerable people, *and* you suspect a body is buried at the location Mister Jago was shot.'

He put the pieces of paper down, picked up the phone and asked the person on the other end for a pot of coffee and mugs. He put the phone down.

'Have I missed anything, Miss Guerra?'

Faced with an open question like that, I had to play it cute.

'I had my appendix out when I was eight,' I said.

'Actually, I doubt if even that is true but you are clearly not a hostile agent; you seem to be an ally so I will treat you as such.'

The door opened and a tray with coffee, mugs, milk and sugar was put on the desk. Once the door was closed, he went on.

'So, I will give you some information because I think you might be able to help us further. We have begun excavating the hollow at the winery.' He paused; it was his big reveal.

'Have you found anything yet?'

'So far, we have excavated to four metres but we didn't find a body.'

I raised an eyebrow but his careful choice of words didn't fool me.

'We have found five sets of human remains. The bodies of five different people.'

Jesus. I was lost for words.

'We are still working to have these people identified. We are looking at dental records but DNA might be more helpful.'

I still had nothing to say.

'Are you alright, Miss Guerra?'

I still had nothing to say. I've been close to death so many times, I've dealt death and will do again but this had come as a shock.

'I'm fine,' I answered. 'Do you know anything about the deceased?'

'Two adults and three children. We believe we may know the identity of the adults but we will wait until we have confirmation.'

'Johannes' farm manager,' I said.

'One of the adults is male so that is possible. The other adult is female.'

'Johannes' wife?'

'We will know soon.'

I took another sip of water.

'And the children?'

'We don't know anything yet. Their approximate age? We can guess at that but it would be just guesses. Our postmortem staff are working to establish what they can.'

I nodded. If they'd been in the ground a long time, the bodies could be just skeletons.

'And this brings me to the point. Why did you make enquiries about Johannes Marula in the first place? Did you have information about his smuggling activities, and were you aware of Damian Hout's criminal involvement?'

This was my big reveal. I leaned back in my chair and I told him about Margaret, about John the Bastard and how he'd stolen money from a number of people before turning up in South Africa under a false identity.

Chapter 54: Laura

Seven weeks later, a guard of honour accompanied us from the hotel to Cape Town International Airport. Nkosi drove our car and Lieutenant General Sorenson, in dress uniform, accompanied us through check-in and security. We stood in the departure lounge where I gave him a hug and Oliver shook his hand. He said we had made things very interesting but, if we ever returned to South Africa, we should look him up. I asked him to keep us in touch with the investigation; he said he would.

Sixteen hours later Oliver and I arrived at my flat at Old Weston, Cambridgeshire. I kicked off my shoes, stretched the travel out of my bones and flopped onto the sofa while Oliver poked about in the kitchen.

'You have nothing to eat,' he called.

'*We* have nothing to eat,' I corrected. 'Anyway, I've ordered. It'll be delivered in a couple of hours.'

‘Take out?’ he asked hopefully.

‘Food shopping, but we can get a take out, if you like?’

He came into the lounge and sat beside me, his body dwarfing mine.

‘Food is good. I’ll cook us something. It’ll be nice to eat home-cooked for a change.’

‘Looking forward to it.’

‘So, do you intend to keep me cooped up here as some kind of a sex slave while I finish my recuperation?’

‘That’s an attractive idea but, tomorrow, we’re going to Hereford.’

‘Hereford? That’s the place where Johannes ripped off your hippy friend?’

‘That’s the place,’ I said. ‘Early start in the morning so let’s chill this afternoon and get an early night.’

‘I’m here for the early night action,’ he said with a smirk.

‘Let’s be careful of those ribs,’ I cautioned, but I was smirking too.

The next day, in one of those rare, magical moments, the pouring rain that had dogged our journey all the way from my flat stopped as the train pulled into Hereford. We emerged from the station into bright sunlight. A taxi from the rank took us to the countryside inn, about eight kilometres southwest of the city where I’d booked us a bed and breakfast for the night.

‘What time is your meeting?’ Oliver asked as we were unpacking. ‘And where is it?’

‘Two pm and it’s downstairs,’ I replied with a big smile.

‘Princess, you really are the best mission planner I’ve ever had.’

‘I know.’

'Modest too.'

'I know that as well.'

He glanced at his watch. 'We've got two hours to fill, you want to do anything special?'

'Yes. I would like to take you downstairs to the bar, get you a drink, sit you beside the log fire and cuddle up.'

He exhaled noisily.

'That sounds like a most excellent plan.'

Two and a half hours later, we were still in the lounge, facing each other over a small dining table. Oliver checked his watch.

'Doesn't look like your meeting is happening.'

I sighed noisily and looked at my half-empty glass.

'I think you're right. If we go back to the room, I'll get the guy's details and call him.'

I looked around the lounge one last time. Nobody new had come in since I'd last checked and none of the people there looked like they might be the guy we were here to meet.

The lounge was half-full: an older couple eating a late lunch, a young couple cooing at each other over half-empty glasses, a few singletons in office clothes, tapping at their laptops or glued to their phones.

'Let's go, big dog,' I said and held out my hand to him.

I followed him up the stairs to the main landing where he unlocked the door and pushed it open for me.

As I walked into the room, the man sitting on the chair in front of the dressing table looked up from a copy of Sporting Life.

'Finally! I've been waiting half an hour for you to get yourself back up here.'

Chapter 55: Laura

With the light behind him, he looked small, thin and wiry. An older man, maybe in his early 60s, with a thick mob of dark hair. Nothing much to look at, I thought, but when he stood, walked forward and offered me his hand, I corrected my first thoughts. He was suddenly taller, thicker and much more powerful than I'd thought.

'You must be Laura Guerra.' It wasn't a question. He knew who I was, just as he knew which room I was in and how to get in without breaking anything.

I shook his hand.

'And you must be Richard Knox.'

'Molly,' he replied in his thick Glaswegian accent. 'They call me Molly.'

I didn't ask why they called him that. He looked at Oliver with a questioning gaze.

'And this is Oliver Jago,' I said. 'He's a good guy.'

Molly and Oliver looked each other over, decided they liked what they saw and shook hands.

'I'm sorry for breaking into your room. I thought it would be easier for us to speak in private.'

'Can I get you anything to eat or drink?' I asked.

'No, thanks, lassie. I ate before I arrived.'

I sat on the corner of the bed; Oliver took the other chair and Molly sat in front of the dressing table again.

'Molly,' I began. 'I really appreciate you being here.'

'It makes a nice change from the gardening, getting out and meeting new people.'

'Gardening is what you do?' I asked.

'I read, I do gardening, I study form.'

'"Form"?' Oliver asked.

'The gee-gees. Horses.'

'Any luck?' I asked.

'I am consistently successful at picking geriatric, three-legged horses with all the get up and go of someone who has gone to the bingo, but it keeps me entertained.'

I launched into the reason for us all being there.

'As I hope my contact explained, we'd like to get some background on someone, Harry Todd, from a person who knew him. I tried getting information on his crash but that's locked down. Instead, I'm looking for some information about Harry from people who knew him. My contact at the Ministry of Defence told me you knew Harry.'

'Well, contacts at the MOD tend to have an official flavour to them.'

'The one thing I need to make clear: this is not an official enquiry. I met Harry's wife. She could do with a little closure. She's knotting herself up inside. Some good words would go a long way to helping her.'

'Not official? A kind of a character reference, is that it?'

'In a nutshell, yes,' I said.

Molly folded Sporting Life in half, tucked it inside his jacket and then stared at me. I felt like I was being lasered.

'Why do you want to know anything about Harry?'

'His wife-'

'Margaret,' he interrupted.

'Yes, Margaret. She has never really dealt with his death. The investigation and the inquest didn't give her any closure. She's still carrying this around inside and, below the surface, it's been eating away at her for decades. I want someone to sit down with her and talk about him. She needs to talk about him, the person, not the cog in the military machine.'

'You know where she is? Margaret?'

'I do.'

'A couple of us tried to find her when we came back from…' He stopped himself. 'When we came back. She had dropped off the radar. We heard she got took up with some civilian from Hereford and then she was gone. Rumour was she'd gone to South Africa with him.'

'No,' I said. 'That didn't happen. She's in Wiltshire, living in a converted horsebox down near Stonehenge.'

'Well, that's a surprise.' He paused for a few beats while he collected his thoughts. 'He adored her.'

'That's the kind of thing that would be good for her to hear.'

Molly nodded, thoughtfully.

'He really did. He lied to her a lot. We kept the truth from her to protect her. He truly adored her.'

'"We"?'

'The troop. The squadron, the regiment. Harry was a popular guy. Really popular. He didn't socialise with us much; spent almost all his off-duty time with Margaret but, on the job, H was the go-to man if you wanted something.'

'You called him H?'

'That and Donkey,' said Molly.

'Donkey?' asked Oliver, joining the conversation for the first time.

'He was hung like one.'

Oliver and I laughed out loud.

'What kind of things did he lie to her about?'

'Operational things,' he said.

I looked puzzled but he didn't explain.

Oliver joined the conversation again. 'What did Harry do

for you guys?'

Molly paused for several beats before he replied.

'H was the best pilot the regiment ever had.' With that one simple statement, I knew that Molly was the perfect man to sit down with Margaret.

'Can you tell her that?' I asked. 'She needs to know her husband wasn't a figment of her imagination. She's trapped in a place in her head where her husband only exists in her memories. She needs to know he meant something to someone else.'

He was silent for what seemed a long time.

'I might be able to get one or two other people to speak to her. I'll definitely do it but one or two other people as well, would that help?'

I sighed with relief.

'Yes, Molly. That would be tremendously helpful. How long do you need?'

'Maybe a week? One has to travel.'

I checked my mental calendar.

'A week would be perfect and there's just one small favour I'd like to ask of you… Could you get me a little something before we leave here tomorrow?'

Chapter 56: Laura

A week later, we were sitting on a bench on the footpath near Bishop's Walk, outside Salisbury Cathedral.

Oliver turned to me and said, 'I've enjoyed our stay in England; it's been a laid-back mini holiday but tell me,

Princess, what's in Salisbury?'

'A loose end,' I replied.

'It's an odd place,' he said, looking around.

'Why is it odd?'

'I just watched you buy a quantity of class A drugs from a respectable-looking market stall.'

'Class A drugs are available in any city, anywhere in the world, if you know where to look.'

'I guess that's so. I didn't have you as a drugs person, though.'

'Oh, they're not for me.'

'For your hippy friend?'

I laughed at the thought. 'No, not for her but she does love a cup of herbal tea.'

We sat silently for a few minutes as we watched the squawking seagulls dive-bombing each other. He changed the topic.

'It's old.'

'It's ancient,' I agreed.

'This city is about a thousand years older than our country,' he said, nodding at the Cathedral in front of us. 'When was that built?'

'Thirteen-twenty,' I answered.

'Wow, that was quick. It's only thirteen-forty-five now.'

'Christ, Oliver. Don't you have any sense of occasion?'

'Occasionally.'

I looked sideways at him. He was actually smirking.

'What are we waiting for?'

'About thirteen-forty-five,' I said. I patted his leg. 'OK then, big dog. Saddle up. We're on the move.'

It took us nine minutes to walk to the footbridge near the

bus station. When we were a couple of minutes away, I called the police then I took the bag of drugs and Molly's 9mm bullet from my pocket. I continued walking. The same gang of youths lounged on the same footpath and were offensive in the same way.

I told Oliver to get his phone out and film everything as we approached them. I held my breath but they didn't disappoint.

'Hey, look,' shouted the big one. 'The immigrants are in town. A black man and his Chinese whore.'

They all turned to look at us.

'What are you filming, dickhead?' demanded the big one.

'You,' said Oliver as his shoulders squared up and he shifted his weight onto the soles of his feet.

'You could film me and the boys taking turns with your slut instead,' he countered.

I walked right up to him, pulled his face down to mine and gave him a kiss on the lips. He pulled back and swung a hammy fist at where my head was but I had moved before he had even swung his hand back. The blow passed in front of my face. His mental processes were slow, his reflexes even slower.

He shifted his balance and began to raise his boot to kick my left leg but I stepped further to the left. When his leg passed through where I had been standing, I grabbed his raised ankle, curved my right foot around his other ankle and hooked it from underneath him. I took a pace forward. He fell backwards and hit the ground hard.

One of his sidekicks came swinging at me. I stepped towards him, ducked beneath his wildly inaccurate head-shot, grabbed the back of his baggy trousers and pulled them down hard. Then, as I stood up, I pulled his underwear down as well.

I turned and faced the remainder of his gang. They all thought they could take me but none of them was willing to try.

I looked to Oliver - who was still filming - and shrugged.

Two uniformed police officers jogged towards us from the direction of the bus station. They asked what happened while the youths all started talking at the same time, mostly jabbering and pointing at me. One of the officers walked over, radio on her shoulder chattering away. She turned it down and asked what happened.

I explained that Oliver and I were walking along when the big lad racially abused us and threatened to sexually assault me. I added that I believed he was under the influence of drugs.

She turned to her colleague and told him to frisk the big lad who had just struggled to his feet. The discovery of a bag of white powder and an unspent 9mm bullet in his pockets had him rapidly placed in handcuffs.

Meanwhile, Oliver was still filming.

The police took our details and asked if we could go down to the police station to make a statement. I asked if that was necessary given what they'd discovered. They said our statements would help.

Meanwhile, the big lad, hands cuffed behind him, was shouting at the police officers about how his father would make sure nothing happened to him.

Oliver said he'd post the video on the Internet, just to make sure something did. Oliver looked angry. The big lad looked furious, his face pink with rage.

Oliver said he would email a copy of the video to the police and we'd visit the station tomorrow to give our statements. Then, we got a taxi back to our hotel on the outskirts of the city.

Later, in bed, he turned over and gave me both barrels of a fearsome stare.

'Princess, we need to have serious words.'

'Do we?'

'Yeah, we do,' Oliver said. He took a deep breath, inflating his impressive chest and slowly let it out. 'You knew that was going to happen. This afternoon. You knew they were there and you knew they would react to us. You may be the best intelligence operative the US has, but your knowledge of this afternoon's fun and games goes beyond having good intel.'

I couldn't answer and I couldn't tell him the truth… Could I?

'You're right, Oliver. I knew that was going to happen.'

'The question I want to ask is *how* you knew.'

'Do you believe in weird shit, Oliver?' He thought about it for a moment.

'Shit happens, Laura. Sometimes it's weird shit.' He paused. 'Yeah, I guess I do.'

'I saw it.'

'In, like, a dream?'

'Yeah, "in, like, a dream".'

'So, you're a witch?'

'No, I'm just me. I just sometimes know things.'

'That's kinda spooky.'

'I'll make your hair stand on end in a minute.'

He smiled. I put my fingers to his lips.

‘You have a lovely smile, Oliver. You don’t show it often enough.’

‘You make me smile more than anyone I’ve ever met.’

I kissed him.

‘I have to go out by myself tomorrow. Will you be able to entertain yourself for a few hours?’

‘I think I can stay out of trouble without you for a little while. Where are you going?’

‘To visit a real witch.’

Chapter 57. Margaret

From my chair, I watched someone begin the long walk up the steep, grassy track. They’d come from the blue caravan down on the bend but, whoever it was, it wasn’t Lisa. The unseasonably warm, late morning sun cast short shadows as it beat down. Whoever it was would be thirsty when they got to me.

I continued my crocheting while I watched them take form. She was Asian. Slight, short but she made speed-walking up the hill seem effortless.

As she drew nearer, I noticed her head was topped by long, dark hair worn up in a way I would never have been able to replicate. She was pretty; her face had probably broken hearts but her deep, dark eyes, much older than her late twenties, told tales of grief, suffering and pain and… happiness, too.

She wasn’t even breathing hard. I studied her face. Mentally, I unfurled her hair and, in my mind’s eye, saw it long, flowing over her shoulders and halfway down her back. The pieces dropped into place.

There was no doubt this was the girl I had seen in my head.

'Hello, Margaret,' she said in a pleasant, quiet voice.

My name came so easily to her, so familiarly yet I knew we had never met. I may have seen her face but I didn't know her name.

She had no bag, carried nothing. I wondered what she was doing here and what she wanted because she was completely focused on me. I continued crocheting the row.

'My name is Laura,' she said as if she had just been inside my head, reading my thoughts. 'Would you mind if I spent a little time with you?'

Her question was perfectly timed. I reached the end of the row, set my crochet aside and looked up at her.

'How may I help you?' I asked.

'Over the last couple of months, I've bumped into a couple of people who, coincidentally, mentioned you.'

Mentioned me? I was shocked.

'Oh? And why were you talking about me?'

'I wasn't talking about you, Margaret,' she said. '*They* were. I met a dying man in Cape Town last month and, a week ago, I met someone in a pub in Herefordshire.'

At the mention of Cape Town, I knew who she was talking about. Another face I had seen in recent dreams. It was a face that belonged to ancient history, a disgraceful episode I had shut far behind me. I didn't want that conversation.

'Hereford?' I asked.

'Someone who served with your husband. A friend of his.'

I didn't say anything. It was like having an out of body experience. Hereford belonged to a life that wasn't mine.

The memories that swam into my head were someone else's, memories not part of my life now.

I didn't know what to say. I looked up. Her smile was kind.

She put her hand in her pocket, pulling out a small box of fruity teabags.

'A peace gift,' she said, offering them to me.

I thought about it for a moment.

'You'd better sit down while I put the kettle on.' I rose from my chair and stepped up into the lorry. She half followed but leaned against the doorway, not coming completely inside.

This felt like an odd situation and yet… And yet I sensed I knew her. Very strangely, I felt comforted by her presence.

I wondered what this young woman had come to tell me.

Chapter 58. Laura

Two mornings later, we drove the hire car to the old cow byre, half a mile from the Stonehenge end of the chalk track on which Margaret's horsebox was parked.

We stopped next to a large Volvo SUV. The windows were down, we could hear people inside chatting. There was laughter and bad language. I saw Molly and gave him a wave as I got out of our vehicle.

The SUVs doors opened; the men who got out were all roughly Molly's age; one used a walking stick, the other three seemed spritely. I shook Molly's hand and he introduced us to David, Jaimie and Lofty. I introduced Oliver. Molly asked if I'd like to give the briefing.

'Thank you for being here,' I said. Harry's widow, Margaret, has been living the life of a hermit for decades. That's not a bad thing and the lifestyle seems to suit her but, because of the way her life went, she hasn't been able to talk to anyone who knew her husband. It may be simple of me to want this one thing but all I would like is for Margaret to be able to talk about her husband with someone who knew him.'

'Is she alright?' asked Lofty who, being slightly shorter than me, seemed to be not lofty at all.

'She's fine and she's mostly very happy but she lost all her savings and, with that, a lot of self-esteem. She leans on her memories for support but doesn't admit it to herself. I'd like to put some extra mileage on those memories, if that's OK with you gents?'

They all agreed.

'Does she need money?' asked Jaimie.

'No. A few weeks ago, Oliver and I met the man who stole her money. We got a refund which I will put into her bank account today but that's a surprise. I'd like it if you didn't mention money.'

There were a couple of nodded heads and an 'aye' from two of them.

Molly asked, 'Got a refund? Just like that?' and sized up Oliver.

Oliver held up his hand.

'Not me,' he said. 'Laura can be very persuasive.'

I changed the conversation.

'Jaimie, are you going to be alright walking down this track with your stick?' I asked

'I'll be fine and, if it's a problem, the lads will sort me out.'

'We carried you to the top of Mount Kent in eighty-two and you still want us to pick up your slack?' asked Molly.

'Are you still grumbling about that? Anyway, Harry ran down, picked me up and carried me up to the top of the mountain. He bloody threw me into the back of the chopper and almost got his arse shot off waiting for you slackers.'

That caught my attention.

'Mount Kent? The Falklands?' But Margaret said Harry never did any ops.'

'Aye,' said Molly. 'That's what he told her. It was his way of protecting her.'

David chimed in. 'Harry was the best pilot the Regiment had. He flew thirty ops for us, maybe more. He even flew occasional ops for the Navy.'

They talked as we walked, mostly reminiscing but also catching up on who was doing what and where they were doing it.

As we approached Margaret's home, I could see she was sitting outside, crochet in hand, but she had put on a smart, floral dress and was wearing a shawl that looked home-made.

'Margaret,' I began. 'These are the gentlemen I told you about. Is it OK if they sit with you and chat, just for a little while?'

'Of course,' she said. 'I recognise Molly and David looks the same as he used to. Hello, Jaimie. Hello, Lofty. I don't know why you've all come so far to see me.'

The four of them lined up to bend down and kiss Margaret on the cheek, then they took seats around the table she'd set out. She made to get up and muttered she'd put the kettle on. I shushed her back into her seat and said I'd do it.

While I was waiting for the kettle to boil, I found Margaret's bankcard in her handbag. I transferred some of the money Oliver and I got from the sale of the Krugerrands we'd found in Damian's Piaggio. Then, the seven of us sat outside her home, enjoying the warm weather and listening to tales of affection for Harry from Molly, David, Jaimie and Lofty.

It was lovely to be there, even if it was just to see the reactions on her face. The four ex-soldiers loved Harry.

And so did Margaret.

Chapter 59. Laura

For the first time since we'd left Nebak, Oliver and I didn't have things to do. Neither of us had an agenda. We could do whatever we wanted and there was nobody we needed to see. But he was still in recovery so we kicked back and took things easy. For a few days, we stayed in the area and saw the ancient sights, but the English weather soon turned so we decided to chase the sun.

We left the UK and settled in a luxurious resort a few kilometres outside Marrakesh, Morocco. For a week, we acted like tourists. We browsed in the Medina, ate delicious food from street vendors, toured the city and ventured out into the North African countryside. During the second week, we became sedentary, barely straying from the pool.

One afternoon, as we lay on our poolside sunbeds, I was beginning to doze when Oliver spoke.

'I have to go to work soon, Princess.'

It felt like too much effort to sit up so I stayed on my sunbed and asked, 'Are you feeling restless and looking for a way to ditch me?'

'No to both of those.'

‘Why then?’

‘I figure, I’m nearly healed now and my money’s going to run out soon. I have to get back to work.’

‘Another six months of no-frat,’ I reminded him.

‘That’s the downside.’

‘What’s the upside?’

‘They pay very well.’

‘Yeah, they do pay very well.’ I thought for a minute then asked, ‘Where did you go? On your last op?’

‘I forget,’ but we both knew he hadn’t.

‘Do you ever think about doing something different? Maybe not doing what we do?’

‘I think I’m like most people. I think about doing something different all the time.’

‘Why don’t you do something different then? You have half the Krugerrands we found on Damian’s airplane. That’s about two-hundred-and-fifty K. That should keep you going, if you wanted to try something different.’

‘I’ve got almost none of that money left.’

I was surprised. ‘What?’

‘I’m giving you half of my share because you gave all of yours to Margaret and I’ll give most of what’s left to my ex-wife because she’s bringing my girl up. So, I guess I’ll keep on doing what I do. That’s why I need to go back to work.’

I didn’t know what to say. This man’s generosity was almost limitless.

‘Well, you can’t give me half of your share. I won’t accept it,’ was the best I could manage. ‘It’s your money, Oliver. What you do with it is up to you but giving any of it to me is not an option. What we brought away from the Piaggio we split, fifty-fifty…’ I paused a long, long, thinking pause.

Oliver broke the silence.

'Come back, Princess!' he called in a mock far-away voice.

I was jerked out of my thoughts. I reached over and slapped him on the backside playfully.

'We've forgotten someone,' I said, sitting up. 'Maybe two someones.'

He rolled over and stared at my breasts. I patted him on the thigh.

'Can you at least try to look at my face?'

'Whatever you say, Princess,' he said, not shifting his gaze upwards.

I pulled the towel up to cover myself.

'Listen to me, you big oaf. This is important.' He propped himself up on his elbows and looked at my face.

'I'm listening. I wasn't *not* listening.'

'You weren't paying attention.'

'I was.'

'You weren't,' I said adamantly.

He sighed. 'Who have we forgotten?'

'There's someone else in Damian's gang. There has to be someone else.'

'Why?'

'The Piaggio Damian and the mountain were making their escape in?'

'What about it?'

'It's the wrong airplane,' I said with confidence.

'What do you mean, Princess?'

'Stop trying to pull down the towel and listen to me.'

He sighed again. 'I'm all ears.'

'Damian told us that, amongst the things they smuggled out of South Africa, there were people. They took those people to Arab countries.'

'I remember that.'

'The Piaggio doesn't have the range for that kind of flight.'

'Maybe they refuelled somewhere?'

'In a straight line, the distance from Cape Town to the Arabian Peninsula is about…' I thought about it for a moment. 'It's about seven-thousand kilometres. In the Piaggio, they'd have to refuel six times to give them a decent safety margin, and that's without carrying a full payload.' I looked at him and watched realisation dawn behind his eyes.

'No. They used a different aircraft; I'd bet tomorrow's breakfast on it.'

'And I know how much you like your breakfast,' he said as he lay back down.

'There's one more thing.'

'What's that, Princess?'

'There has to be more people involved. At least two. I think we've met one of them.'

'We have?'

'I'd bet my brunch on it.'

'That's a big bet! So, what do you want to do about it?'

'We could email the Cape Town police and tell them what we think.'

'You've certainly got contacts down there now. You would probably get taken very seriously.'

'Or we could go back to South Africa and-'

'Do the job of the local police force?' he finished the sentence for me.

'Yeah.'

'Is this a game to you? Because, you know, I got shot just

a few weeks ago.'

'I know and I feel very bad about that.'

'But you still want to go back to South Africa and kick somebody's ass.'

'I do because of those flights. But you don't have to come with me. You could stay here or go back to the States and I could join you there?'

'Join me there?'

'You know. If you wanted. If you didn't mind.'

He didn't owe me anything and yes, he was right: I was the reason he got shot. I felt guilty about that and, every time I saw his ribs or his patched-up shoulder, I felt worse than guilty.

I decided I was going back to South Africa and, when I found the other people involved, I was going to make them pay for my guilt.

Chapter 60. Laura

Two weeks later, we arrived back in South Africa, a little jaded and ready for bed. We'd flown from Marrakesh to Amsterdam where we spent a week doing the sights. Then, we took a direct flight from Schiphol to Cape Town.

I checked my phone. Surprisingly, there was a voicemail from Margaret. I listened while Oliver picked up the hire car.

Laura, it's Margaret. Molly gave me your number. All of that money you put into my account... there's such a lot of it. It can't all be mine? I don't know what to do with that. Also, Molly told me to say hello to you. He said a mutual friend looked you up and you are one of the 'good guys'. What does that mean?

I rang her back but my call went straight through to voicemail. My message was swift and simple.

Hi, Margaret. Thank you for getting in touch with me. The money is yours. John was dying and had nobody else to leave it to. I think he had a deathbed epiphany. Please give my regards to Molly.

Oliver pulled up in the hire car.

'Where to, Princess?' he called through the open window.

'Let's deal with the crap tomorrow. Just drive north out of Cape Town. I've found us a nice, out-of-town hotel where we can have a shower, a meal and get some quality mattress time.'

'All of those things tick the right boxes with me.'

'As soon as I get you on a mattress, I'll tick another box for you.'

He didn't reply but the smirk on his face lasted all the way to the hotel.

He was still smirking the next morning when we pulled up in front of the office at the Independent Flying Club.

'Oliver, here's the plan. You're not at full fitness so I need you to hang back and be eyes. When I go into the office, you check out what's going on around here. Tap on the window if you see anything that makes you uneasy.'

He grunted.

'I'm not used to hanging back.'

'I'm not used to having someone with damaged ribs and a recently patched hole in their shoulder and lung on the team.'

'You've put me so far back I'm not on the team, I'm still in the dressing room.'

'And lovely it was to watch you dress. I'm out of here. Count to twenty and do a slow walk around.'

'Princess, are you expecting trouble?'

'Not at all,' I sort of lied. 'I'm just being cautious.'

He grunted once more.

I got out of the car and walked to the back window of the office. It was so dirty that I wouldn't have been able to see anyone in there if they were playing floodlit table tennis.

Around the front, the door was unlocked. Nothing seemed to have changed inside. Well, that's not completely true. Everything looked untouched but the boots weren't up on the desk and the wearer wasn't around.

I checked the movements board. No aircraft were scheduled in or out.

I stepped back out just as Oliver walked casually around the side of the building.

'Anything?'

'Nobody in.'

'Shall we try the mobile home?'

'I can barely contain my excitement.'

I walked to the front door while Oliver faded towards the rear. I was about to raise my hand to knock when the door was pulled open. The same brown boots, the same denim jeans and the same Australian Bushman's hat. The shotgun pointing at my stomach was new though.

'Well, this is a surprise.'

'Is it, though?' she asked.

'Absolutely. I didn't think I'd get greeted with a shotgun when I came to ask about flying lessons.'

'Where's your friend?'

'Resting. He had a serious injury'.

'I heard about that. So, there's just you?'

'Just me, yes. So, about that lesson you mentioned?'

'Lady, I've seen you fly. I saw you take off and land the Piaggio. You're no amateur. In fact, you could probably teach me a thing or two.'

She eased the shotgun barrel upwards a few degrees, the business end now pointed at my chest. It was cocked and ready to fire. The thing with shotguns is they're dangerous, even in inexperienced hands. Her hands didn't look inexperienced.

Her eyes never left my face and I wanted to keep her mind off pulling the trigger.

'What do you mean, you've seen me fly?'

'The minute I saw the Piaggio take-off. And later, when it landed, I knew Damian wasn't at the controls.'

'It is a lovely aircraft.'

'You'll get one more ride in it.'

'My friend knows I'm here.'

'That's OK. You won't be here much longer and neither will I.'

That wasn't what I wanted to hear. I'd already mapped out her weak points but I needed to keep her talking. The shotgun tilted the odds against me.

'When did you start?'

'Moving things?'

I nodded.

'Damian and I started in the late eighties. Johannes changed things. His farm meant we had storage.'

'So, you stored whatever you were moving up at the winery and, when you had enough for a full load, you brought it down here in wine tankers.'

'Well, you've got it all figured out, haven't you?'

'But you flew it out in something else.'

'You really do have it figured out.' She stepped back into the room and, without taking her eyes off me, lifted a jacket from a wall hook. 'Time to go for a little ride.'

She walked towards me, the shotgun still pointing at my chest. I took tentative steps backwards and out of the doorway.

'We'll walk across. Turn around and head for the big hangar.'

I raised both arms, crossed them over my head, palms to the front, turned around, and started walking across the airfield.

'There's no need to do the fancy surrender thing. I know I've got you.' She didn't have me. She just didn't know it yet. I kept my hands where they were. Oliver would know the special forces signal for 'do not interfere'.

'Where's the aircraft with the range to get you to the Arabian Peninsula?' I asked as we walked.

'My, my. Damian really did blab the whole story.'

'We needed something to talk about.'

She didn't answer for a few paces and I really wanted to know. Maybe she was weighing up what she could tell me and eventually decided she could tell me everything. That's when I knew she was going to kill me regardless.

‘Botswana.’ After a few more paces she continued. ‘Damian owns a ranch there. It’s a big spread with a dirt airstrip, just a short hop in the Piaggio.’

‘I’m guessing you flew the other aircraft?’

She gave a small laugh.

‘Damian could barely fly the Piaggio. He tried the C-One-Thirty a few times but it was too much for him.’

‘A C-One-Thirty?’ I asked. ‘That’s a big, expensive aircraft.’

‘It didn’t cost much. It’s older than I am. We bought it from some rebels in Angola who had liberated it from someone else. Originally, it belonged to Ethiopia but it changed hands a lot before it got to us.’

‘Why did Nala shoot Oliver?’ My quick change of subject caught her off guard for a moment.

‘You were too close to the old bottling plant,’ she replied. ‘I think she panicked. She thought you might have found evidence of what used to go on there. The place is covered with sensors and alarms; you would have triggered them as soon as you got out of the car.’

‘And she was in on everything?’

‘Not at first. When the farm manager found out what was going on, he told her about it. She told her father and he confessed their farm and whole life was tied up in the scheme.’

“The scheme”. Two simple words to sum up human trafficking, people smuggling, child abuse and slavery.

She went on.

‘The farm manager accidentally discovered the warehouse when it was full of people.’

‘Children,’ I corrected.

‘Whatever.’ Her off-handedness made me want to hurt

her. 'Keep walking.'

'So, she killed the farm manager?'

'No. Johannes told Damian. Damian killed him. Nala was cool about it all, though. She has expensive tastes.'

'*Had* expensive tastes,' I corrected her.

I reckoned I had almost all the information I needed so I slowed my walking pace. The large hangar was very close now.

'How did you get involved?' I couldn't believe how ordinary the conversation sounded.

'Damian. He's my brother. It was his scheme from the beginning.' I slowed my pace some more. 'Which one of you killed Damian?' she asked.

'Me. I shot him. He was still alive when we threw him out of the Piaggio but we were a hundred kilometres offshore. He wouldn't have lived long.'

'I'm going to do the same to you. Then, I'm going to the ranch in Botswana and nobody will ever find me.'

She jabbed me between the shoulders with the barrel of the shotgun. I stopped walking and she jabbed me again but the blow glanced off my back because I'd already begun turning fast to my left. I caught and held the barrel in my left hand, directing it down and outwards. She pulled the trigger but the loud shot raised a cloud of dust a few metres away. I kicked her between the legs and, a split second later, pulled her head hard down onto my knee.

She tried to shift her balance. She was fast, wiry and fairly fit but I was faster, a whole world fitter and better trained.

As her brain registered the damage to her face, I shifted to my right foot and kicked her legs from underneath her. She started to fall so I jabbed the shotgun into her side and helped her to the ground with a knee to her throat. In less than two seconds, she'd lost control and was now a bleeding, groaning wreck of pain and smashed bones.

I looked back towards the airfield building. Oliver was leaning against the wall, dusting his fingernails on his coat like an office worker who had just stepped outside for a breath of fresh air.

Chapter 61. Laura

'What do you want to do today?' he asked.

'Can I be honest?'

'Totally,' he replied.

'I'm bored with airports. I'm bored with flying. I'm bored with going there and I'm bored with doing that. What I want to do is sit on my ass and do nothing. I want to have no plan other than to ask people to bring me things I want to have brought to me.'

He looked at me over his sunglasses.

'That's quite demanding.'

'I'm feeling demanding.'

'Also, a little bit lazy.'

'I'm feeling very lazy. Pass the factor fifty.' He handed the bottle over and placed it on my stomach.

'There is, of course, just one flaw in all this.'

I sighed heavily because he was right.

'I know.'

'The police officer walking towards you right now,' he said to hammer the point home.

'I know!' I said in fake annoyance as I struggled up off the sunbed.

Constable Nkosi offered her hand and her trademark smile. The youth she pulled along with her looked a mixture of surly and curious.

'How are things in the South African Police Service today, constable?' I asked.

'Business is booming. Excavations continue at the winery. Sad things have been unearthed but that work will go on.'

'I'm glad it will go on,' I said and I was. The people buried there needed to be identified and properly laid to rest.

'Johannes' solicitor had paperwork giving a share of the winery to someone in England. We've been in touch with her. She says she doesn't want it and she's going to sell it to you for one Rand. The paperwork wasn't signed but our legal people say it'll probably come to you anyway.'

That was unexpected.

'And the other things?' I asked.

'Detective Damian Hout's workload is being investigated. We won't know where that investigation will lead us for some time, but his sister has been charged with multiple offences. She's in a prison hospital, waiting for trial. Someone else waiting for trial is Sampson Low.' She looked at me with a mischievous grin.

'I don't know that name.'

'He's an old man now, retired. He used to work for the civil service.' The penny dropped.

'Would he be the man who supplied Damian with new IDs?'

'Indeed. It would seem there were many false identities. We are trying to work through a list of such people.'

I nodded. It was logical that Johannes wasn't the only person who had received a new identity from Damian. I wondered how many other people Samson Low had supplied.

'It certainly seems you've been kept busy. And you? How is the flexitime working out?'

'It's wonderful. I have so much time banked that I could take a couple of months off and not lose any money.'

I gave Nkosi a broad grin.

'I'm very pleased for you. You deserve to reap your rewards.'

'Speaking of rewards… You asked us to find this one?' She pushed the young lad forward. I ignored him for now.

'Has he been bad?'

'Two thefts from tourist hotels and an attempted car theft in Jo'burg. His college tutors said he was bright but he hasn't amounted to much since he left education.'

I looked at him for a few moments. He shuffled awkwardly and wouldn't meet my gaze. He knew who I was. He was probably wondering what influence I had with the police, to have him picked up and brought here.

'Hello, James. How's your face?'

He didn't answer and kept his gaze on the floor.

'Constable Nkosi, could you take his handcuffs off?' She gave me a questioning look.

'James, don't try to run away. I want to talk to you.'

For a moment, I thought he was going to spring into action but he shifted his balance from foot to foot then settled.

'Sit down, James,' I said, pointing to a chair under the sunshade next to Oliver. 'Would you like something to drink?'

He shook his head but sat on the edge of the chair.

'Who do you live with at Da Gamma Park?' I asked.

'Uncle,' he said.

'Just your uncle?'

'Sister,' he answered.

'How old is your sister?'

'Twenty-three.'

'And how old are you, James?'

'Twenty-five.'

'What did you study in college?'

'Computers.'

'Are you any good at it?'

He shrugged.

'What does your sister do?'

'Book-keeping.'

'And your uncle?'

'He works on boats.'

'So, he's away a lot?'

He nodded.

I opened my book and took out the debit card I'd been using as a bookmark. I handed the card to him.

'Yours?'

He looked at it and nodded.

I picked up my phone and pressed a bunch of numbers.

'I've just put some money into your account,' I said. 'It's not a reward; it's a part payment for something you're going to do for us.'

'What thing?'

Before I answered I turned towards Nkosi and asked, 'Is he currently wanted for any crimes or misdemeanours?'

She shook her head.

'In that case, James, make yourself comfortable. I'm going to offer you a job.'

I turned to ask Nkosi if she would like to stay while we

talked when something slammed into my chest. I had a burning pain like someone had shoved a red-hot poker through me and I looked down at the hole just above the line of my swimsuit. It leaked blood and then I couldn't breathe any more. I fell sideways, Oliver caught me. There was shouting and running and the day turned to night and I heard Oliver shouting some more.

Chapter 62. Six Months Later

From the front page of the Cape Town Bugle

KILLER GUILTY

Anthony Kreller (35), a former detective with South African Police Service, has been convicted of the shooting of an American tourist.

Kreller had shot Ms Laura Guerra (28) as she sat at the poolside of her hotel in Constantina, Cape Town. The trial heard that Guerra had been instrumental in the discovery of the bodies of three children and two adults at the Cape Heartland Wine Estate. Kreller was heavily implicated in those killings. The court was told Kreller killed Ms Guerra as an act of revenge.

Some weeks prior, Kreller had been plucked from the sea by an Australian fishing boat. He had been taken to Durban where he was hospitalised and treated for various injuries. He disappeared from hospital and remained undetected until he shot Ms Guerra.

Kreller will be sentenced next week. He is expected to receive a life sentence. The court gave a special commendation for bravery to police Constable Nkosi, who apprehended Kreller.

A statement from South African Police Service confirmed that Kreller was a former detective. The statement also said Constable Nkosi will receive a service award for bravery and has been promoted to Sergeant.

The End.

Brennig Jones was born and raised in the Welsh Valleys, has been around the world a bunch of times, lived in Spain a few years and is now based in the East Midlands (UK) with his wife, two step-children, four spaniels and four cats.

Storm is Brennig's third novel, and second in the *Tempest* series.

Brennig can be contacted through his website: brennigjones.com